THE CORT CHRONICLES BOOK 2

Spirral

S0-BYG-169

David D. Bernstein
ILLUSTRATED BY VICTOR GUIZA

outskirts
press

Dedication

I want to dedicate this book to all the families who have lost loved ones to the COVID-19 epidemic. Keep their memories alive.

Table of Contents

Chapter 1
The Rescue

One Week Later

Andy woke up from his dreams of hope. The cell room was bare; the flashing red light had settled. His body felt normal again. In front of him hung a nineteen-inch plasma TV. Where did it come from? Was he transferred to a different cell room? Everything seemed the same. The last thing he remembered was being punished with water and light. He could not recall how he got here or when. The TV was turned on from a distance.

"Good morning, Andy 8, did you sleep well?" He was looking at the face of a woman. Andy started to remember. It was the Ms. Weed 2 person. It was she who humiliated him; it was she who tortured him. Finally, things were beginning to make sense. Did he have that brief amnesia period? Maybe it was because of the torture he experienced. Andy wanted to smash his fist right through the TV, but he knew he had to control his temper and act like a perfect boy.

With a fake smile, Andy said, "I slept very well, Ms. Weed."

"Have you learned your lesson, young man?"

"Sure have," Andy said calmly. "Thanks for the cool shower. I really needed it."

"You certainly did, young man," Ms. Weed answered. "That is a good lad. Now it is time to go to your new room and meet your roommate."

After those words were uttered, the cell door swung open, and two robots grabbed Andy. They were solid steel and they moved around the room swiftly on gray and black wheels. Andy could not believe how strong they were. His body was lifted easily. Their grips were rock solid. Andy figured there was no point in fighting, especially for an eleven-year-old boy.

He was carried through endless hallways, several turns, and passed by empty rooms. He could not believe how massive this prison was. After several minutes, they approached an open room. It was the size of a medium closet, had two full beds, a square thing that looked like a sink, and a large hole in the floor. Andy guessed it must have been the bathroom. He was surprised that these machines knew so much about human needs and wants. He was taught back in school that machines were controlled by men, but here machines controlled and owned men. His body was thrown inside, the door was locked, and the robots rolled away.

Andy was able to get a closer look at this room. The floor had black and white tiles that felt like ice under Andy's bare feet. He assumed they were watching him 24/7. Ms. Weed 2 did tell him to forget about all privacy. He noticed the TV hanging above his head. He wondered if he could catch some earth shows here. Most likely not. It probably was another of those brain-washing machines like he saw back in CORT City. This time he had no protection with him. He got up, still feeling the pain from his forced landing. Thankfully, it was just a large bruise on his butt. Andy started pacing back and forth.

After about twenty minutes or so, the door was thrown open and another boy, probably about Zack's age, was dropped off, and the door locked. Andy looked up at the newcomer; he had blond hair tied in a ponytail, hazel eyes, and large glasses. He was wearing the same see-through uniform that Andy had on. It was wet and very see-through.

"Hello," Andy said.

"Hey. Looks like we are roomies," the boy declared.

"What is your name?" Andy asked.

"I am John, and who are you?"

"I am Andy."

"I heard about you from my resistance captain. Such a pleasure to meet you," John said, holding out his hand.

Andy grabbed it and gave it a nice strong shake. "A pleasure to meet you."

"You said you were with the resistance. How did you get captured?"

"I was on a secret mission for my captain and messed up badly. Before I knew it, I found myself being humiliated, abused, and tortured."

"Looks like we are in the same boat."

"Yep, I guess."

"What kind of things did they do to you?"

"Since I am part of the resistance, they tried everything from whipping to using drugs and beyond, the whole time. They tried to make me speak and give up all of our hideaways."

"These creatures have no mercy."

"The things I saw here break all the rules."

"I do not think rules exist here," Andy said.

"Not in the outside, but in Icy City, there are many rules," John continued.

"What is Icy City? I haven't heard of it before."

"All I can tell you is that it's the last human city left in my world. I cannot go into details because, you know." John pointed his finger at all the mirrors.

"I understand," Andy said. There was a strange moment of silence between the boys. They stood face-to-face, looking at each other's see-through uniforms.

Underground War Room

Wendy gathered all her resistance leaders to come up with a plan to take down CORT Academy and to save Andy from its grips. Zack was part of the group.

The room looked like an abandoned station. A plaque still hung here with Williamsburg Station engraved on it. A large oak table stood in the center. A few old paintings and photos covered the walls. Those pictures represented the world long gone. Images of people walking on the large streets with baby strollers, pictures of vendors selling hot dogs and peanuts, and beautiful buildings long gone.

"We must come up with a plan," Wendy started.

"Do you have the manpower to take the school down?" Zack questioned.

"I might have a few seeker weapons that Melvin gave us."

"How do we know where Andy was taken?"

"I chipped your brother right before he disappeared."

"Is everyone chipped?" Zack wondered.

"Yes, and from what my tech crew says, he is with another of the resistance members."

"Wow, that sounds good."

"Perhaps by now, both were humiliated, tortured, abused, and who knows what else. Yet it is still good news that the chips have not been found. This gives us about three days to take them both back," Wendy said.

"Why so little?" Zack asked.

"It takes ten days for the old chip to be deactivated and another five days to put in the new robot chip."

"What is that?" Zack asked again.

"It is the chip that is inserted in the children they capture."

"Once that happens, then what?" Zack asked.

"It basically means that CORT has won the battle," Wendy said.

"We must hurry," Zack said.

"Here's the plan," Wendy said. She took a pencil and turned the map over. She started drawing. "We need a small group to go in. The only way we can succeed is to blow up the school's central computer. It controls everything."

"We need two individual groups to go in. One must keep the guards engaged and the other must use the tunnels. Our target is Remake school two." Wendy drew a large red X on the map. "That is where the latest signals from the chips have come from. The tunnel goes right under it."

Zack could not believe how smart the girl was; he could see why she was the leader. He started to fade into a daydream of Wendy and him going on a date. He finally woke up when he heard: "We need volunteers. Each group will have six people in it. I will lead one and Jackson will lead number two."

Zack watched as resistance members started to step forward. When Zack tried to move forward, Wendy pushed him away.

"We cannot lose you, Zack."

Zack tried to reason, but he knew deep inside that Wendy was right. He had to trust the resistance. He did not forget how they saved him.

"Okay, I will stay here," Zack agreed at last.

"Sounds like a good plan," Wendy said with a smile. "We start our mission at daybreak." With those words, the war room cleared.

The Next Day

By the time Zack woke up, the place felt like a ghost town. Did the groups leave? Why was nobody here? Did Wendy know what he was planning?

Zack got up, put on his one-piece armor suit, and

grabbed his weapon. He walked out the door and started heading down the tunnel. He was surprised at the complete silence that surrounded him. How would he find them? He did not know this place. All he could do is wait to hear voices; maybe they would guide him to the proper location. The moment he turned his back, he felt a hand grab him on his shoulder. He was about to strike his weapon but heard a familiar voice.

"Dude, do you really think I was going to leave you behind?"

Zack turned around and saw Wendy standing behind him. With her were five young people.

"Don't do that again."

"The number one rule is never turning your back."

"Was it a training exercise?" Zack asked.

"You can say that" Wendy said. "Now, let's go and save your brother."

Zack joined the group, and they continued the journey.

"What is our job?" Zack asked.

"Our job is to save your brother while the other group will cause the shutdown of central computer," Wendy said.

"How will we know when the right time comes?" Zack asked.

"This is what you will use." Wendy reached into her pocket and handed Zack a strange device that looked like a mixture of cell phone and a walkie-talkie. It was the size of Zack's hand, and had a green stripe with the words "Resistance East" on it.

Zack took the device and looked at it closely. "How does it work?"

"You press this button and speak. It has a two-hundred-foot range."

Zack pressed the button and called out, "Testing one, two, three!" He could not believe how loud this little device was. Everyone in the group was carrying one.

"Let's go," Wendy said.

"Where to?" Zack asked.

Wendy gave Zack a glance and it said everything. The group settled in and headed down the tunnel. They soon arrived at a large stone door.

"Our ride is just beyond there," Wendy said.

Wendy reached into her pocket and pulled out a large keychain with four ancient keys on it. She placed her finger on the wall, and instantly a keyhole appeared. Next, she inserted the smallest key and turned right. The door swung open.

"What is that Wendy?" Zack asked.

"It's our ride to Remake Academy 2," Wendy said. The small group entered what looked like an elevator shaft. Several chairs with seat belts were inside. Colorful ads were posted on the wall: "Smoke Carmel Cigarettes and Live," "Drink Milk and Grow Strong," and "Just Do It." Zack looked around the little room and smiled. For the first time, this place reminded him of home.

"Okay, guys, grab a seat," Wendy said. She sat in the first row and buckled in. The rest of the group followed her lead. Zack sat in the third chair. Next to him was a boy who looked no older than ten; his left hand was holding a teddy bear and in his right hand he held a large, curved knife. It was like a scene from a horror film. A girl with an exceedingly long ponytail that reached her ankle sat on his other side. She must have been thirteen. Her whole-body suit was covered with knives and sharp stars. Zack decided not to say a word to them. The children literally scared him. He could only imagine how much bloodshed they had seen in their short lives. Zack was the beginner here. The other two kids in this group looked normal to him and, of course, there was Miss Wendy, who Zack thought was hot. He did not say a word but drifted into thinking about her. One thought about her made his face turn red like a tomato. He tried to hide his face with one hand. Suddenly, Zack felt a kiss on his cheek. It came from the girl with the long ponytail. He heard a distant giggle coming from somewhere.

"I wanted to do that so badly," a sweet voice said. At that moment, a realization hit Zack: this would be his team, and only teamwork would make good things happen.

"That will be enough, Heather," Wendy said.

"I was just having my fun, girl," Heather responded.

Zack watched as Wendy opened a panel next to her chair, took the second largest key, and turned it. Suddenly, the room started humming, and puffs of air came out from the walls. After some smoke, the room took off. Zack could not tell in what direction they were heading. It reminded Zack of the Disney ride called "Space Mountain." He understood the reasons for the seat belts. They must have been flying at 200 miles per hour. After a couple minutes, Zack heard a squeak, and the transportation device came to a very sharp stop. Zack felt his stomach drop. He threw up his whole meal. He heard kids laughing all around him.

"What was that?" Zack asked, turning red again.

"You just learned an important lesson: do not eat too much before a trip," Wendy said.

Water came out from all sides and washed away the food junk.

"We are here, guys," Wendy said. The sound of seat belt buckles opening filled the small space. After everyone got up, the door in front of them swung open.

"Thank you all for riding the Pink Flood Express and watch the gap," Wendy said as everyone stepped down.

Still recovering from the wild trip, Zack stumbled from side to side. It was the first time he felt his leg limping. He did not feel the ground under him. It was an amazing rush that ran through Zack's body.

Slowly, Zack adjusted. They heard the first explosion from the distance.

"Okay, guys, that is the signal. Weapons out and move forward," Wendy commanded.

As soon as Wendy's words were heard, the group sprung forward. Zack could not believe how fast they moved. He tried his best to stay close.

"Stay together!" Wendy yelled.

Five minutes later, the second explosion rang out. The tunnel echoed loud, and all Zack heard was Wendy's distant voice calling, "Go!"

Zack and the group made it to a staircase. They climbed the ladder as one, but it took them five minutes to get inside a rather large building. At the end of the journey, Zack saw lots of gray ash everywhere. Flashing red lights and large warning signs were floating above them.

"We will self-destruct in ten minutes," a metallic voice announced.

"Hurry, hurry!" Wendy called.

The team worked fast as lasers, metal stars, and knives flew. Swords banged, and chaos was everywhere. The battle of man versus machine had started. Tin cans, iron parts, black wheels, and iron dust scattered everywhere. Zack watched in amazement at the coordination and speed with which those children worked.

"Go find your brother. We got this," Wendy commanded.

"Yes, boss!" Zack called. He took off, destroying some roller robots in his way.

"Eight minutes and counting. Clear out, everyone," the robotic voice said.

Each door Zack passed was wide open, so he continued to run forward. He hoped he would survive and not get lost. As Zack moved, he heard voices coming in front of him. He was surprised because

Andy and a few more children in wet and clear-white uniforms emerged and bumped into him.

"Andy!" Zack screamed.

"Bro, hey!" At that moment, the two brothers embraced each other with tears pouring down.

"Five minutes before self-destruction," a voice called.

"Come, follow me," Zack said.

The group of children and Andy smiled, and Zack led the way he came. He saw lots of ash everywhere. It was hard to tell who was human and who was a robot. He hoped the group that came with him was all right. Zack noticed Heather and Wendy nearby.

"I have found him," Zack said.

"Hi, Andy," Wendy said with a smile.

"Hi, Wendy," Andy answered.

"This way, guys and gals!" Wendy announced.

Just next to her, a door was opened.

"Hurry," she said.

"Four minutes to the end," the voice called.

The children leapt into the open door and ran as far away as they could. A countdown started: "Ten, nine, eight, seven, six, five, four, three, two, one."

When that ended, they heard a massive explosion that rocked the tunnel.

Finally, everything collapsed, and entrances vanished under piles of rock.

"How many survived?" Wendy asked as the group gathered next to another solid wall.

The count began, and the total survivors from the

group was only seven out of eleven. Zack was happy to see that none in his party had died. In addition, twenty children from the school stood around them.

"It looks like seventy prisoners had been transferred to another school," a young boy said.

"Fifty robots have been destroyed," said Heather.

"We did okay tonight. We will honor our fallen back at headquarters," Wendy said.

With tears in her eyes, she pressed the wall and another keyhole appeared. Taking out her large keychain, she chose a middle-sized key and opened it.

"This is Green Flood: it is larger and can hold thirty." When the door opened, Zack noticed thirty chairs with seat belts.

"Buckle up, everyone," Wendy said.

Soon, twenty-seven children were sitting. Heather decided to sit next to Zack. Most of her metal stars and knives were gone. The simple armor looked so weird after the attack.

Zack looked at all the faces around him. All twenty children—twelve boys and eight girls—wore see-through uniforms. Zack had never seen so many almost naked bodies in his life. He could only imagine what these poor kids went through. He had so many questions to ask his brother but decided to wait until later. He would have more time together with him. Like before, Wendy pressed a button and, once again, the transport took off.

It took them just an extra five minutes. When the

machine stopped, this time there was no laughter, but pure silence. Everyone left the transport in a single line. The age range of the children was five to eighteen. Zack could see the exhaustion in everyone's faces.

Wendy broke the silence. "Everyone who was rescued, go to our infirmary. Please take the injured people." The kids looked over at Wendy. "Zack, you will help them. It is time you learn how deadly this civil war is."

Zack had no words. Heather joined him.

"I will show you where," she said. She grabbed Zack's hand and pulled him behind her, and the twenty children plus four fighters followed closely behind them.

Soon, Zack came to a familiar place. It was here where he woke up over a week ago.

Joy was overjoyed to see him.

"I was told that you will be assisting us," she said with a smile.

"I guess so," Zack said.

"You must put these on." She handed him a white coat, paper mask, and plastic gloves. The staff in the hospital were fourteen people of all ages, and thirty beds were scattered. Five were used for injuries and twenty were available for those rescued.

"Go on and help these poor children out," Joy said.

"What do I do?" he asked.

"Observe for a minute and get to work," Joy replied.

He watched as people helped the released prisoners undress and put on something that looked like hospital robes. He noticed some weird machine being used on the bodies.

"What do I do with this?" Zack wondered.

"You must see if any of the children have chips implanted in their skulls or other body parts," Joy said. "We only have fifteen minutes before they are reactivated from CORT Headquarters. If that happens, we will be found and destroyed."

Zack worked fast. Children were placed face down on the bed, and he had to literally strip each of them. It did not matter if they were male or female. Some of them had chips in their skulls, others in their back, and others had them in other areas on the body. The machine worked easily. In those fifteen minutes, Zack pulled out five chips from three boys and two girls. The machine was cool: all he had to do was press a button and the machine grabbed the chip from the body and crushed it to dust.

Joy had to help Zack with the stitches. Together, they saved five children. The three boys were nine, eleven, and sixteen. The girls were seven and ten. The next step was to give them physicals and help them out. A few of the kids shook wildly. They received iodine shots, which eventually relaxed them. While he was working, Zack discovered that when he touched an injured area on the body, his hands felt a tingle in them and, in many cases, small cuts and slashes just vanished.

"Zack, you are special. It has been at least four years since we had a healer, here," Joy said.

Zack could not believe his ears. Did something here give him healing power? How had he not noticed this before? It was the first time Zack felt special.

Chapter 2
Spirral

Word spread quickly of the fall of Remake School. It was the first time that CORT felt danger lurking and biting at the door.

A little dirty and ripped, Ms. Weed 2 moved back to Headquarters, and so did seventy children who were taken out the moment the alarm sounded.

She stepped in front of the CORT computer council, which consisted of three exceptionally large computer faces. The energy shock hit Ms. Weed 2 hard and she fell to her knees.

A loud voice spoke in her head: "How did you dare fail us? We should be more powerful than those weak humans."

"Master Smith, they snuck up on us through unknown tunnels. They had new powerful weapons."

"Ms. Weed 2, I need a full report. Speak up or I will short-circuit you." Another energy shock hit her.

"Remake Academy 2 has been fully destroyed. We lost a hundred loyal robots and twenty of our students."

"Ms. Weed 2, can we track them?"

"I have tried, Smith, but the chips have been removed and destroyed," Ms. Weed 2 said.

"Can we rebuild the school?"

"No, master, all of our equipment has been turned to dust. The school is terminally destroyed. They even got the backup files."

"Nothing is gone," Smith said.

"How come?" Ms. Weed 2 said.

"I have backed up all that was built in my files. I will transfer them to your system."

"Yes, Master Smith."

"You should be able to rebuild in two years. Until then, I must speak to Daddy and his Elders. You are dismissed. You will receive everything tonight." With those words, Smith went silent, and darkness filled the space. Ms. Weed 2 walked back to her room, still feeling the shock she was hit with.

The next day, Smith sounded the alarm to call an emergency meeting of the Halibuts, the top leaders of CORT Central Inc.

The meeting took place in the basement of CORT Central.

"Mr. Smith, this better be important," a man with long white wires and gray dead eyes said.

The Elders themselves consisted of three males and two females. Each of them controlled an area of CORT Earth.

"It is critical, Daddy," Smith said. Two other computer systems also lit up.

"Speak to me, son," the man said.

"Yesterday, CORT Academy 2 fell to the resistance, and I fear we must activate project Spirral AI, or we will all fall in this war."

"How dare you speak to me like that! We are way too powerful to lose!" the man screamed.

"I have been calculating all kinds of possibilities and formulas, and they all look grim for us," Smith said.

"It is bad news. Your calculations are usually spot-on," Daddy said.

"I recommend you vote on activation of the project," Smith said.

"I trust your views, my son, and I will call for a vote now," Daddy said.

As soon as the comment was said, all five hands went up together.

"Smith, you win. The activation of the project will begin tomorrow."

"Thank you, Daddy," Smith said.

"I will put you in charge and give you access to all needed resources. Just tell me what you need, Smith," Daddy said.

"I will need one thousand human slaves, three hundred engineers and computer programmers, a small army, and all necessary resources to build Spirral."

"It is done, Smith," Daddy said.

"Thank you, Daddy."

"I will upgrade you after the meeting."

"I will be ready," Smith said and went dark.

During the next thirty minutes, details were discussed and planned.

Daddy said, "Sam, you will take over Smith's job and, Sandy, you will be programmed to do your job and Sam's old job."

"Yes, sir." Both faces spoke together and went dark.

The last words of the meeting were: "Operation Spirral AI activated." After that, the room cleared.

Chapter 3
New Magic

After everyone was healed, Zack and Andy finally got to catch up on everything they went through. It had been five days since Andy was captured and several weeks since Zack came here.

The brothers sat next to each other at dinner. John sat next to Andy.

"I want to welcome all our new recruits to our home," Wendy said. "It was a great victory for us. Sadly, we lost three heroes in the battle."

The names and pictures appeared on a huge whiteboard. Cheers and tears filled the dining hall. The three children lost were ten, thirteen, and fifteen. Each of their biographies was read, and they were honored. The bodies were never recovered, but the plaques were crafted. Wendy got up and marched over to a large wall filled with the names of the people lost over the course of the civil war.

In large letters was written "Hall of Heroes." When she came back to the dining hall, Wendy stood in front of the people and called forward the twenty names of those who were saved. Each of them stepped forward and told their stories from the time they were captured to the present.

As each child spoke, cheers filled the room. Yet, Zack sensed a lot of sadness all around. Andy came close and for some reason he was happy. Zack understood why.

"Thanks for saving me, bro," Andy said.

"I couldn't let my little brother die," Zack said.

After the cheers, the room fell silent again. It was both a day of celebration and a day of mourning. Zack could only imagine all the death and suffering Wendy had seen in her sixteen years. At least he had a childhood with school, sports, friends, etc. Wendy had nothing but war almost her whole life. She had to go through heavy training for six years and probably did not know where her parents, friends, and family were. How could anyone do this?

"Earth to Zack," Andy said.

Zack looked up at his brother's smiling face.

"Yes, Andy, I am here. Sorry to drift."

"I want to introduce you to someone," Andy said.

"Who is that?"

A boy stepped closer and put out his hand. "I am John," he said.

"Who is this?" Zack asked.

"He was my roomie," Andy said.

"Nice to meet you. Hope you took care of my bro."

"Yes, I did," John said.

"If you did not, I will punch you out," Zack joked.

The three boys stood together in a different room. Zack did not even know how he got here. It looked very modern and had a massive central altar surrounded by endless weapons: axes, guns, swords, sticks, and other strange devices. He did not know if this was real or a dream. To his left was Andy; on his right was John.

"What's going on here? Where are we?" Andy asked.

"It does not surprise me," John added. They heard a woman's voice coming from the front. The boys looked up and saw a rather large woman with snow-white hair and deep brown eyes. It felt like she could see deep into their souls.

"Welcome, young ones," a loud, scorching voice called.

"Where are we?" Zack asked.

"You lads are somewhere between reality and death. You are between dreams and nightmares," she said.

"How did we get here?" Andy asked.

"You have opened the passageways; it has not been done in decades," she said.

"What passageways?" John asked.

"That I can't say," she called.

"What does it mean?" Zack asked.

"My name is Martha. One day we will meet personally."

"You are right in front of us," Andy said.

"Is that so?"

It was at that moment Andy tried to grab Martha, but his hand passed right through her.

"What do you want from us?" Zack questioned.

"You three are the chosen ones. You, Zack, can heal," Martha said.

"What can I do?" Andy asked.

"How about me?" John interrupted.

"That is for you two to find out on your own," Martha said.

"What do you mean, we are the chosen ones?" Zack insisted.

"It means you three and one more will save us, save me," Martha finished.

Zack could not understand what she meant.

Within minutes, he found himself and the other two boys on their knees. Their bodies froze.

"What are you doing to us?" Zack demanded.

"Here, I am in charge," Martha said softly.

"What are we supposed to do to go free?" John asked.

"Just sit and watch. You three must be cleansed by the waters of Lake Gold."

Suddenly, the floor below them collapsed and a lake swallowed them. The water felt warm and glimmered like gold.

The three boys woke up back in the underground. They were on the cold floor. Six eyes opened as one. Their eyes were glowing. Each boy felt an awesome power shiver through his body.

"Was it all a dream?" Zack wondered.

"I also had the strangest dream," Andy added.

"Me too," John called.

Zack's body felt wet. Andy and John looked at each other and noticed their one-piece suits were soaked.

"I do not think that was any dream, big brother," Andy added.

They held each other's hands.
The small drops of blood blended with each other.

Zack could not believe his eyes. Here he was with two other boys all wet and shivering. It meant they had a bizarre connection to each other. Where they came from, the term used was "blood brothers." What was about to take place? Who would be the fourth? These questions and several others raced through his head.

"What the hell was that?" John asked.

"To me, it looks like all of us are connected," Andy said.

"Dudes, that was so weird," Zack added.

From that point on, Zack understood that destiny had come upon him. A human bond between the three boys had begun. Everything happened for a reason.

The three boys went back to the food hall where Wendy had just finished talking. Zack looked up at her and noticed she was soaking wet like he was. The rest of the people in the room looked dry.

Could it be coincidence or just error? Zack wondered. Could Wendy be the fourth of this fellowship? When did she get a chance to go through Lake Gold? All this was so odd. A connection had bound the three boys, and Wendy could be part of their group. Zack's whole body was shivering. It was not only his wet uniform, but the idea that such an amazing teenage girl would be with him. He wondered if she would notice him and treat him like a boyfriend. Back in Trinity, New York, beautiful girls just looked away from him. He barely even had any friends.

The three boys stood next to each other as Wendy

finished her speech. This would be the perfect time to ask her the big question: if she experienced what the three boys went through. The three suits still clung to their bodies, and the wetness made them feel extremely uncomfortable. The way they were so see-through did not help either.

They watched the last of the room clear up and distant footsteps of people faded. The silence was scary. Wendy walked toward them.

"What happened to you guys?"

"We have the same question for you," Zack stated.

"Let us all talk in my private chambers," Wendy said.

The four children looked at each other and walked down the hall. This was the first time they would be seeing Wendy's room. Maybe when they got there, Zack thought, he would get to know her better. *Mom used to say that a room tells a lot about a person.*

They soon entered a rather large space. On the floor were several leather chairs. In another corner, a queen-sized bed with rose-colored sheets and an ancient-looking dresser stood erect. All the walls were covered in newspaper clips, photos, and old magazine articles. Each of them had pictures of beautiful people, both male and female. In another area were twelve television screens with images of different areas of the underground. It was probably a security feature to help look over everything.

"Welcome, boys, to my room. I have some extra uniforms for you," Wendy greeted them. She walked over to the dresser and brought back four new uniforms. Like she did not care, she stripped off her old uniform and threw it in a white box.

The boys tried to turn away, but their eyes were focused on the beautiful young woman standing in front of them. It was obvious what they had to do.

Andy, Zack, and John also took off their wet uniforms and threw them in the same box. They did not move for a few minutes but looked at each other. Zack and the other boys turned red for a moment, but soon the embarrassment left them. They finally dressed in silence.

Wendy said, "Finally, dry clothing." She acted like nudity was common here.

Zack could not believe how strange everything was. He was in a parallel world and maybe here this was a common thing. It was like the whole concept of privacy was meaningless. He did understand how cultures varied from place to place. It surprised him how everything he was taught vanished in one moment.

"I saw the same thing you did," Wendy said.

"You mean, you met Martha?" Zack asked.

"Holy cow," Andy called out.

"I guess our group has gathered," John said.

"Looks like we are all connected by fate," Wendy said. "If Martha asks you to do something, you better do it."

"Is this Martha a queen here?" Zack asked.

"No, Zack, she's more than the queen: she is one

of the last three Oracles in my home. Not one person dares to go against her," Wendy said.

"If she is so powerful, why can't she save everything?" Zack asked.

"Her powers are great, but CORT's powers are greater," Wendy said.

"What now?" Andy asked.

"We need to finish the bonding ceremony," Wendy said.

"What do you mean?" Zack asked with fear in his voice.

"You will see soon. After it is done, we will leave for Eastview."

"What do we do now?" Andy asked.

Wendy went back to the closet and brought back a small knife. "I think in your world it is known as blood bonding." Wendy slightly cut her finger. John followed and did the same. Eventually, Zack felt a small knife slash him, but it felt only like a mosquito bite. Andy was the last in line. Once it was done, they held each other's hands. The small drops of blood blended with each other; strong, deep heat flowed through Zack's body. Zack heard a voice in his head. It was Martha's.

"The ceremony is complete, and now you are bonded with your bloods. The new connection is what we call inner magic. You are now enriched with gifts. Zack, you have healing; Andy, you can now control elements; John, you have speed; and Wendy, you have foresight. In addition," the voice went on, "together, you children of men will connect through mind, heart, and love. Together, you will quest and stop a living darkness from being created."

Soon, the voice was gone, and Zack's life flashed quickly by. The last vision was of many people being whipped, tortured, burned, and stripped. It reminded Zack of a picture he once saw called "Hell." Everything went silent and, once again, Zack found himself in Wendy's room holding hands with the others. He could tell that each of them was sweating as if they just had been in a hot sauna. A new surge of energy filled him.

"It is done. Tomorrow, we will travel together," Wendy said.

Zack never felt anything like this before, but he started to cool down. When he heard a voice in his head, it surprised him. This was his brother's voice.

"Hey, bro, what's up?"

Zack could not believe it. He looked over at Andy, who was quiet and smiling. It was the day Zack learned that the four of them could communicate both in words and through telepathy. He had to try hard to keep his thoughts about Wendy out of his mind and only in his heart. Tomorrow would be the beginning of a journey to save CORT Earth.

Chapter 4
<u>Going East</u>

The next day, the alarm clock went off early. It was 5:00 a.m., the old-fashioned alarm clock showed. Zack woke up right away. He heard a very loud knock on his door. He opened it and saw Andy and John in front of him. Both were carrying matching backpacks. Zack found the same backpack near his bed. He looked inside and found four pairs of boxers, flint, rope, extra uniforms, a pair of brown shoes, a first aid kit, and a pocketknife. He looked around and found other necessities like a comb, two toothbrushes, and a couple of toothpastes. He also packed his weapon lying nearby.

"Hello, big brother," Andy said.

"Hey, little bro," Zack said.

"I discovered how to use my gift last night," Andy boasted, smiling. He raised his left hand and a small whirlpool of water appeared out of nowhere. It danced around and landed on Zack.

"Come on Andy, you soaked me!" Zack screamed. The other two boys laughed a little.

"Don't be such a Grinch. It will dry up in a couple of hours," Andy said.

"I also learned my gift. I have been practicing a few hours," John said. He took out a dagger and slashed through the air extremely fast. In one minute, he did thirty slashes.

"Those gifts are so cool," Zack called. Soon, he heard a familiar voice coming down from the hall.

"Now, boys, stop showing off. Each gift we were given will play an important role on this journey."

Zack looked up and saw beautiful Wendy heading toward them. She approached and gave each of them a hug.

"We will leave in about one hour. Let's get some breakfast," Wendy said.

They headed down the paved hall to the dining area. The smells of fresh-cooked food filled the air. The kids entered the dining hall. A table set for four was waiting for them. Out of the three children who were saved in Remake Academy, two were ready to serve them. Zack recognized one of the girls he helped back in the hospital. The table itself was full of all kinds of food: cold and hot cereal, bacon, ham, hot drinks, many types of bread, cheeses, meats, and much more. Wendy went out of her way for this meal.

The children sat down and were treated like royalty. The servants, one girl and two boys, helped. This was probably the best meal Zack ever ate in his life.

The feasting went by fast. Wendy stood up and said, "Okay, my blood brothers, we have to leave now." The boys stood up and headed to the tunnels. Wendy made sure to take extra rations for the journey.

Zack did not know if he would see the underground or his family ever again. At least he had his little brother beside him. They entered an elevator and soon found themselves outside. Harsh winds were blowing in their faces. In addition, a rotten smell was haunting them. They saw an ancient field in front of them. Dark twisted glass and metal glistened under the orange sun. The winds bit them badly.

"Can you do something about that, Andy?" Zack asked.

"I will try," Andy answered. He raised his hand and dirt arose around them. It stood up briefly and finally hit them in the face. It tasted like old tar and an itch began.

"What is the staff?" John asked.

"Be careful with that," Wendy warned. "It is extremely dangerous, and it is not soil." The itching got worse. It felt like poison ivy times ten.

"What is happening?" Andy called out, scratching hard.

"We are covered by human and robot ash. Many battles have taken place here." Still itching, Wendy used all her strength to grab a lotion from her backpack. "This will help." Wendy took some on her finger and placed it on her face. The redness and itching stopped. Eventually, she was able to put this lotion on the others. The boys were happy to get relief. The redness and swelling started to go down by the second.

"Andy, you must never use your powers in the center of a street like this or other ghost cities," Wendy said.

"Got it, boss," Andy answered. The party continued to walk. It was a quiet street.

Wendy closed her eyes for a moment to activate

her power. "We are about to be attacked. Weapons ready," she warned.

As the kids turned the corner, they spotted five rolling robots heading right at them. Thank goodness for Wendy's warning, they were ready. During the first minute, six rockets missed their heads by inches, hitting a building structure 100 feet away. The building crashed on the ground, and plastic, steel, and glass scattered everywhere. Zack and Andy looked in amazement as John's pair of daggers slashed quickly. He moved smoothly with sidesteps and flips. In a couple minutes, two of the five robots had become dust. Wendy foresaw every move seconds before. It looked like she was doing a ritual dance with the machine. Zack smiled and ducked as a tentacle arm almost took him out. Andy raised his left hand and a small twister appeared. He threw it at another robot who was lifted high in the air and slammed down to the ground, turning to dust. Wendy did a flip in the air with perfect timing, hitting the robot on the back and destroying it. Zack took out the last one with his collection stick by short-circuiting it. Finally, silence came back.

"We were lucky: it was a patrol, and I am not sure if a distress signal had been sent," Wendy said.

"Is everyone all right?" Zack asked.

Think so! three voices sounded in his head.

Telepathy is cool, Zack thought. He sent a message to Andy: *Are you okay?*

I feel a bit tired, bro, but I think I am all right.

As those words filled Zack's mind, Andy collapsed in front of him.

"Oh no!" Wendy screamed. "It looks like Andy has been bitten."

"With what?" Zack asked.

"It's a poison that slows down the person until they go into a dream state and sometimes never wake up."

"What can we do?" Zack asked with concern.

"You must use your power. But first we must find a temporary shelter. The poison must be drained within minutes or your brother will die."

In front of them, Zack noticed an old storefront. The glass was gone, but the structure was intact.

"Let's hurry. We only have five minutes!" Wendy waved and together they picked up Andy's little body and took him inside.

The structure reminded Zack of a drugstore. It was small and did not seem to have any life in it. Wendy took out something that looked like an ice pack. "Hurry, Zack, you must find where he was hit," she said. Zack took off Andy's uniform, leaving him in his boxers. He saw a large black mark right in the center of his brother's small chest.

"That's it," Wendy said. Zack lifted his hands and placed them on the spot. He put all his love for his little brother into it. Tears fell and memories of them together flashed before his eyes. The dark spot started to disappear, and black ooze started to appear in a puddle near Andy. After a few more minutes, Andy's breathing came back. His face color started changing and the breath of life was brought back into his body. Zack heard some coughing and Andy started to breathe normally.

"We almost lost you, Andy," Wendy said. She placed the ice pack on his forehead.

"We should rest here," John insisted.

"Yes, I agree. We can leave in three hours," Wendy said.

Zack grabbed Andy in a bear hug, and his tears began to clear.

"You saved my life again, Zack," Andy whispered and fell into a deep sleep. Zack fell asleep next to him. John followed their lead while Wendy stood guard over them.

I will not lose them again. Do not worry, old man. I will protect your grandsons with my life. I failed too much already; I will never forget how you saved my life back then, Wendy remembered in her head, trying to make sure that no one heard her. She knew that the connection they had put them in the same boat. They had to save this planet together. She was sensing that a major evil was being created somewhere deep in the darkness beyond Eastview. They had to get to that place soon.

Right before the quest, Wendy learned through her scouts that thousands of people had been disappearing lately from the controlled cities. People had disappeared before, but not at such a high rate.

Soon she heard her companions' voices. They were finally awake. Andy was once again dressed in a fresh uniform and seemed to be back to normal. The other two boys seemed to be rested now. The party gathered for a meal of rations and a few berries. After eating, they were ready to go on the next part of their journey.

Zack was the first to get up. He was incredibly happy his little brother was well. Now he knew what Wendy meant before the journey when she said that each gift would be useful.

Things were once again looking hopeful, and Zack wanted to get to Eastview badly. It seemed that time itself had gotten short. Zack got up and the others followed.

"Doing aright, Andy?" Wendy asked.

"Better, thanks to my bro," Andy said, tapping Zack on the shoulder.

They continued to walk and soon they came to something that looked like a gate that was pulled open and destroyed. In front of them, they saw a rather large pile of stones.

"How will we get out of here?" Andy asked.

Wendy smiled and said, "Things are not like they seem." She put her finger on one side of the rock, a red light flashed, and the rubble moved aside.

"That is so cool. How does that work?" Zack asked.

"Each resistance leader has access. Do not forget humans have been here way before robots ever were." Those words told Zack everything, and kind of gave the resistance an advantage. After the wall swung open, the children found themselves in a wasteland that seemed to go on forever.

"You will need these," Wendy handed each boy something that looked like a gas mask. She took one for herself.

"What is it?" Andy questioned.

"They are called Breathers," Wendy said.

"It is a very trendy device that the resistance uses," John added.

"What does it do?" Andy wondered.

"It helps keep out all the chemicals in the wasteland and turns tainted air into breathable air," John explained.

"Without it, people will basically be dead," Wendy said.

"It was created by our ancestors from Icy City," John said.

Zack got the idea, so he pulled the mask on. He was surprised at how light it felt. It had small breathing holes cut into it.

"The Breather will help you guys, as the wasteland does not have the cleanest air," Wendy shared.

The wasteland was an endless desert. It felt ridiculously hot and steamy. The bright orange and pink sun was hanging over the land.

"How long will our trip be?" Andy asked.

"Last time it took me hours of walking," Wendy said.

"How will we survive in this heat?" Zack asked.

"We sleep in the daytime and travel at night. We must always have our eyes open too," John added.

"The wasteland is a dangerous place; we must stick together to survive," Wendy said.

The exhausted friends walked for a long time through the never-ending desert. Suddenly, they saw a large lake and many green trees. It was a gift from God.

"I usually rest here before I travel," Wendy said.

"How does it remain so protected?" Andy wondered.

"Before magic was lost, about three years ago, the last sage created the sanctuary. He is one of three scattered in the wasteland," Wendy said.

"So, the rumors about hidden areas are true," John added.

"Yep, they certainly are. Though, only a few can see or enter this place."

"How much time will we have here?" Zack asked.

"We should have about seven hours before it gets dark enough to travel," Wendy said.

They entered the sanctuary. It was a beautiful place. It was amazing how such a place existed in a wasteland. The moment the children passed through the entrance; their bodies had been scanned. They were met by an older man.

"Good to see you again, Wendy," he said.

"I was passing by. Here are my friends, Warren."

"Yep, our scanners have already told us. It is a pleasure, boys," Warren said.

"Wait a minute, how can a scanner already tell who we are?" Andy said.

"Sorry I did not tell you earlier, but when you came here from your home, I checked you into our system.

It is only shared with Icy City and all the resistance groups," Wendy said.

"How did you know who we were, anyway?" Zack asked.

"Your grandfather told me about you when he came here about six years ago," Wendy said.

"You mean Grandpa was able to travel through portals?" Andy asked.

"He not only traveled through them, but he was able to create them somehow," Wendy said.

Zack and Andy looked at her with surprise on their faces. They had no idea Grandpa was able to do that. They forgot to ask him. Tragically, he vanished about two years ago and was never found.

"Welcome to the Hidden Town," Warren welcomed the group. "We will do all we can to help you get to Eastview."

"Thank you, sir," Andy said. The children took off their masks. It was wonderful to be unmasked; they felt so relieved to do this. Zack looked around. The town was paved with stones. A small lake nearby sparkled under the sun.

The children were tired even though they barely walked at all in the wasteland.

"Follow me," Wendy said. The town looked normal. It reminded the boys of home. They followed Wendy down the street, and soon they approached a solid brick structure. In the wind, a sign, "Hidden Inn," swung back and forth. The boys also noticed paper scattered around.

"This will be our stop," Wendy said.

"I am very hungry," John complained.

"The last time I was here, the food was amazing," Wendy added.

"It still is," a voice called out.

The boys watched as Wendy ran over to a large black man with a bald head and hugged him. "Ben, it's wonderful to see you again."

"It has been a long time, Wendy. You have grown." Ben hugged her.

"What are you talking about? Last time I was here was one year ago," Wendy said.

"One year and two months to be exact."

"You are still the counting type."

"Of course, I am! That is my gift, and it helps pay the bills," Ben said.

"How is Mary doing?" Wendy asked.

The boys looked over at the towering man as he started to cry.

"Mary died seven months ago. Her sickness took her. I tried everything to save her, but it all failed."

"So sorry to hear that," Wendy said.

"Yeah, life happens," Ben said.

"Ben, these are my friends, Andy, Zack, and John."

"A pleasure to meet you boys," Ben said, putting out a large hand.

Andy placed his little hand out and gave the man a shake. Three of Andy's hands could have fit inside the man's hand. The other boys followed Andy.

"So, the same room plus one," Ben said.

"Yep, that should do," Wendy said.

She took out some papers and handed them over to him. It must be the currency used here. Zack remembered the same had been used back in the dog food factory.

"The pleasure is mine," Ben said. He pointed inside the inn.

The boys entered and sat at a large table. A young boy came over and placed some wooden bowls and spoons in front of them. He went to the back and brought out a large steaming pot. He went back one more time and brought over some hot bread and butter.

"Enjoy your meal," the young boy said. He went around checking on the others in the inn.

Wendy served each boy a few spoons of what looked like stew. Huge chunks of meat, potatoes, carrots, and a green spice of some kind filled their bowls.

Zack took a spoonful and smiled. "Wow, this is amazing."

The other boys looked over at him and dug in.

"Yes, this is Ben's special rabbit stew. You will never find anything like this in the whole world," Wendy said with smile as she also dug in.

It felt so great to be inside the inn. It was so cozy and comfortable. Several large tables were everywhere. Half of them were full of all kinds of people. Everyone was talking and having discussions. Not one person raised his or her voice or swung a fist or kicked anyone.

Zack could not believe his eyes. The outside world was in the middle of a civil war and inside here, peace and love were alive. He looked over at Wendy and asked, "How can people be so nice when the world around them is falling apart?"

"That is a great question, Zack, but there is one simple answer. Everyone here is fighting the same enemy: CORT. We are all human; it is those two things that connect us all."

"How many of these hidden cities are here, anyway?" Andy asked.

"We know of only three. If there are others, we haven't discovered them yet," Wendy said.

After they ate, Wendy handed the young boy a few notes. Zack politely read what it said: "Two crisps. This is legal tender for all human purchases here."

What a strange name for money, Zack thought. The young boy bowed down to Wendy and went back to work.

The party had five deep hours of sleep.

Wendy woke them up. "Everything is ready for us."

"What do you mean?" Zack wondered.

"We have found a ride."

"Do we need our masks?" Andy asked.

"Yes, we do. We will be going through the wastelands by carriage. Ben told me of a hidden road that has not been discovered by CORT yet," Wendy said.

They got up quickly and went over to the gate on

the far east of Hidden Village. They saw Ben standing near a carriage.

"It has been a pleasure to meet you guys." Ben hugged each child and opened the gate. Zack, Wendy, John, and Andy got in. Inside, the carriage was extremely comfortable. Red velvet and silk covered the seats. A few more bags of goods were around them.

"When we get to Eastview, you must present these iron cards to them," Wendy said. "It is a kind of fake ID used there."

The carriage took off and within eight hours, the party found themselves heading toward a large brick, iron, and wood wall.

Chapter 5
Eastview

"Hello," the voice said. "Insert IDs here." The children watched as a drawer came out. It reminded Zack of the bank drive-thru back home. Each kid placed the metal ID into the slot. Instantly the drawer opened and inside they found four handheld scanners and their IDs.

"Thank you," a robotic voice called, and the front gate opened. The carriage pulled inside. The door closed behind them, and they found themselves in the center of a large crossroad. The streets were wide and straight, and the town looked like a mini version of New York City. It was much gloomier and a less busy place. Instead of beautiful window shops, huge TV screens hung everywhere. It reminded Zack of the city they visited before. Once again, Wendy handed the boys the sunglasses.

"You will need them," she said.

A man approached them. "Welcome, merchants. Would you like a spot on our market to sell your goods?"

"Yes, please," Wendy said.

"Come along. You know that five percent of all sales go back to the city."

"Yes, indeed," Wendy said.

"Follow me." The man waved.

The party's carriage followed the man left, right, and straight.

"You can unload here," the man said. He gave the children three merchant cards and left. They found themselves in a large square surrounded by many people unpacking all kinds of goods.

"How do we sell here?" Andy wondered.

"It is simple. Each buyer has a scanner, and all transactions are recorded and taken out of a central account," John said.

"The scanner is also used on our merchant cards, and the sale is credited to our IDs," Wendy added.

"It is like a digital credit card. Very cool," Andy said.

"On our way out, our IDs will be scanned again and five percent from our total sales, plus a ten-dot rent fee, will be taken off," Wendy said.

"Wow, that is a lot," Zack replied.

"Do we have a time limit?" Andy asked.

"We only have three hours," Wendy said.

"How will we find Martha?" John asked.

"She usually finds us. Now, unpack the boxes," Wendy commanded.

At that moment, Zack, John, and Andy took out seven boxes from the carriage. They placed them on the ground. The last items they took out were three large tables.

"What are we exactly selling?" Andy asked.

"We are selling furs, silk, and cotton clothing," Wendy said.

The children continued to unpack. The merchandise was amazing.

"Where did you get them?" Zack questioned.

"A friend of mine picked them out for us," Wendy said.

Soon, everything was set up. There were coats, scarves, hats, T-shirts, and so much more displayed in front of them.

Soon, the children noticed other merchants gathering around them.

"What is this place named?" Zack wondered.

"It is called the Eastview flea market; it happens twice a week here in the town." Soon, the children were surrounded by several merchants. There was barely any room to move.

"What a perfect spot to meet Martha," Andy whispered.

People started to walk in between the merchants.

"I had no idea that even in a robot-controlled world, markets still existed," Andy said.

"It is their way of making life normal. In the CORT world, people really don't belong to themselves. They do not have free will but live under a dictatorship. They are under constant control," Wendy added.

"How do they do that?" Zack asked.

"There are two kinds of controls. One is with hand implants and the other is with TV's," Wendy explained.

"So, no one is free here," Andy said sadly.

"You can say that, but the resistance brings them hope," Wendy said.

The first customer came up to them. It was a woman with long white hair.

"I am looking for two silk skirts and a pair of fur socks," she said.

"We do not carry socks, but we do have an extra fur skirt," Wendy said.

A large smile appeared on the woman's face. Within seconds, the party vanished from the market, leaving behind human androids that looked like them. The real group found themselves in a wooden cabin.

"Hello, Wendy, good to see you again," the woman said.

"Indeed, it is, Ms. Martha," Wendy said.

Zack could not believe his eyes: this was the same woman he saw back in the underground. This time she was real.

All around them, they saw plants, dried herbs, and other strange items.

"We only have two hours," Martha said.

"Did you leave the clones?" Wendy wondered.

"Yep, it looks like you never left," Martha added.

"Great, will they still be able to sell our goods?" Wendy asked.

"They should be fine; my magic has never been broken."

"Wow, so in our place there are clones who look exactly like us?" Andy asked.

"Yes, Andy," Martha said.

"They actually are able to sell?" Zack inquired.

"How, have you heard about us?" Andy asked.

"Your grandpa was very vocal about you," Martha said.

"No one believed him, but just in case, many got ready," Wendy said.

Besides the herbs and strange items, the room itself had a large oak desk in the center, a queen-sized bed, and many photos of the boys' old memories. Each image was iconic. There were old beach photos, large buildings, and even a few photos of the boys standing next to Grandpa in different places they visited. It was like Zack and Andy's childhood had been brought back. It was sad to see what they had lost.

"It looks like you have been following our lives a long time," Zack said.

"Yep, your grandpa was a great man who told me everything about you."

Zack remembered how Grandpa used to talk about everything, both private and public matters. Zack thought back to that day, just about two months before Andy vanished, when Grandpa left and never returned. Tears filled Zack's eyes as those old images came flowing back. Yes, he and his brother were close to Grandpa, and that day he vanished, both of their lives were changed and destroyed forever.

"I can see your grandpa's loss really changed you," Martha said.

"Yes, it did," Andy said and gently wiped his tears.

"It is those memories that play an important part of magic," Martha said.

"How is that?" Zack asked.

Suddenly, a beam of bright light came from her hands and within minutes, the dead plant came to life.

"Emotions plus control and focus equal power," Martha added.

"How do we do that?" Andy asked.

"Choose a moment in your life that was emotional. Focus on that point in time and finally activate your ability."

The boys watched as Martha closed her eyes. They saw some tears come down her face and finally she walked toward a dead plant nearby and touched it. Suddenly, a beam of bright light came from her hand and within minutes, the dead plant came to life.

"Awesome!" Zack called out. "You have the ability to bring living things from the depths of death."

"Correct. I am the last one on this planet with this gift," Martha said.

"Wendy mentioned other sages. Where can we find them?" Zack wondered.

"I have no idea; I have not heard from the others in years. If I ever learn anything, I will let you know," Martha said.

"Did they each have powerful magic?" Andy asked.

"Yes. One had the ability to kill anything with his powers and the other was able to kill and resurrect anything that was alive," Martha said.

"Does anyone know where they are?" Zack asked.

"Nope, but if they are in CORT's hands, they can be used as weapon," Wendy added.

"Indeed, they can," Martha agreed.

"Let's get down to business. Why did you bring us here?" Wendy asked.

"Yes, of course. I forgot that our time is limited," Martha said.

The party watched as Martha walked into a different room of the house and came back with a small bottle and handed it to Wendy.

"What is this?" Wendy asked.

"This, darling, is what I call my Root's potion. It has the ability to break free from any plant that exists on this planet." Martha handed a map to Wendy. "This map will give you the ability to see where you are."

"Thank you, we will find great use for these items," Wendy added.

"There is one more thing I must share with you."

The party listened as Martha recited a riddle:

Three items you will need to discover your path: a wand, a stone, and a mirror. The first will be found only after you stare death in its face, the second will be found in wonder, and the third will be found deep inside a swamp. Now journey, darling ones, and seek what lies hidden within.

After those words were said, the party found themselves once again selling goods on the market square. The rush had slowed, and the sun was setting. It was glowing as it disappeared, leaving darkness behind. At that moment, several streetlamps were turned on.

Shortly, the robots came by and said, "Everyone has to leave. The market is done. Make sure to check out."

The party packed away the leftovers and got back

on the carriage. They left from the west gate. Their cards were checked one more time and the gate was opened.

"Do we need the masks again?" Zack wondered.

"No, not now. The next area has been cleaned and we can breathe," Wendy said.

"Do you know where we have to go?" Andy asked.

"I know of one such place where we will face death, Old York," Wendy said.

"How far?" Zack questioned.

"We are about seven hours away," John interrupted.

Wendy took out the map. She was surprised to see a large green dot with several small red dots around it. "Old York is north from here," Wendy called.

Chapter 6
The Sages

Zack was happy to be out of Eastview. Being there felt very dark, gloomy, and uncomfortable. Just to see all those lost people made him happy to be free. At least he had his brother and friends beside him. He could not believe that Martha had been following him and Andy for such a long time. If she could see the past, there might be a way to get home. It added another mission to his list, but after all he had gone through, a hopeful goal was not such a bad idea.

"We have to head to Old York," Wendy called.

"Are the red dots enemies?" Andy wondered.

"Some could be, others may not be," Wendy replied.

"Can't you use your power to see who is?" John questioned.

"It is not that easy. I am new to all this magic stuff," Wendy answered.

The carriage was moving slowly, and Zack felt cold air swirling around him. At least he was able to breathe normally again. Those masks never felt comfortable. The unpaved road gave Zack's legs great pain, and his body felt like it was being hit by a rock rapidly.

"What kind of road is it?" Zack asked.

"Based on the map, the road is named Cracking Road," Wendy replied.

"I understand why: my whole body is in pain," Zack complained.

"Stop being such a baby," Andy stated. "To me, it feels like a rough massage."

The carriage continued to move in silence. The scenes merged into each other. It was hard to tell the difference between water and land. Zack was surprised that no one they passed attacked them or noticed them.

"What is going on here?" Zack asked.

"I have a feeling that we are still under Martha's protection," Wendy said.

"She is a very powerful sage," Andy called out.

"Thank you, lad," Martha's voice sounded in his head.

Andy could not believe his ears.

"Guys, did you hear that?" Andy asked the others.

"Hear what?" Wendy was surprised.

"I heard nothing," John added.

"Are you going crazy?" Zack asked. "I heard zero."

"Only you, Andy, can hear me," Martha's voice sounded again.

"What did you do to me?" Andy demanded.

"It is one of the powers you have: a connection to me and other sages throughout history."

Andy looked up and saw five faces of the sages above him. He saw Martha and four others. His body shivered as he felt the fantastic power flowing through them.

"How is this even possible?" Andy wondered.

"I am not sure," Martha answered.

"Who are the other four?" Andy asked.

"Sorry, let me introduce you," Martha said.

After Martha spoke, the four voices followed.

"I am David, sage of the moon."

"I am Kevin, sage of the sun."

"I am Zoey, sage of death."

"I am Ellen, sage of death and life."

"Where are you anyway?" Andy questioned.

As one, all five said, "We are lost in the mirror world except Martha!"

"What am I supposed to do?" Andy asked.

"Once you solve the riddle and claim the pieces, you will free us all, Andy. You are our only hope," Martha said.

"How could I do this? I am just a kid."

"No, Andy, you are not. You have the soul of the sage of time. We lost him a century ago," Martha said.

"How will I be able to do that?"

"You have great power to unlock and once you do, great things will happen."

"All of us will always be with you, and one day we will meet," the five voices sounded as one and went silent.

Andy kept everything to himself. Through the rest of the journey, nothing much happened.

Soon, they approached a rather large wall. In large letters, the words "Old York" were floating eight feet above a brick gate.

"Where do we enter from?" Zack inquired.

"We need to sneak in," Wendy replied.

"Do you know the way?" Andy asked.

"I do," John called. "I passed by here on my mission."

"Didn't you get caught?" Zack asked.

"Yes, I did, but it was not here," John answered.

"Lead the way," Wendy declared.

"Yes, ma'am," John answered. The group followed John and ran to the back. The sun was setting in the distance and for the first time in their journey, the children noticed rainbow stars in the sky.

"What is that?" Andy asked, pointing to the sky.

"That is a rare event. How lucky we are!" Wendy exclaimed.

"How often does that happen?" Zack questioned.

"I think it happens once every ten years. When I was six, I also saw those stars," Wendy said.

"What are they called?" Zack wondered.

"I asked the same question. Bob, my leader, told me they are the rainbow galaxies. It is believed that if anyone ever lands on them, they will discover a utopian world."

"What happened to Bob?" Andy wondered.

"Four years ago, he invented a ship and decided to try his luck to get there," Wendy said.

"Did he ever make it?" Zack asked.

"Nope. A week later, one of our patrols found his body."

"How sad," Zack said.

"Sadness becomes a part of the package when you live here," John added.

John stopped in front of what looked like a sewage grate.

"What is that?" Zack asked, but he stepped back when a stream of black smelly water poured out through the cracks.

"Is that what I think it is?" Andy asked, covering his nose.

John smiled. "Get ready to be messy and smelly."

"Are we going through a sewage pipeline?" Zack asked.

"It is the best way to get in," John said. He pulled the lid away. A horrible smell poured out. The boys never expected to walk through the sewers.

"The masks will be very helpful here," Wendy said. The party did not think twice but grabbed their masks and vanished into the darkness.

Chapter 7
Old York

It was good to have masks on since the party sensed the dirty and smelly water soak their suits. It came from below but dripped from the top. They could only imagine how smelly it must have been. Probably if it were not for masks, they would have fainted. With each step, their suits became stickier.

They moved slowly through the sewer. With each step, the disgusting water got deeper and deeper. Eventually, it reached the stomach area. Andy, being the smallest among the group, got the worst of it. After about an hour of walking in the filth, the party saw a ladder attached to a wall.

"Here we are," John said.

"Where will it lead?" Zack asked.

"If we climb the ladder, we can exit into a back alley," John stated.

"How long ago were you here last time anyway?" Wendy wondered.

"It must have been at least one and a half years ago," John said.

"I better look before we get out," Wendy said while activating her gift.

The boys watched as she closed her eyes and stood in silence for five minutes.

"It is not clear if robots are out there or not."

"I will take care of that," John said.

"How will we get through?" Zack questioned.

"Andy, your element control powers will help us," Wendy said.

Everyone watched as Andy climbed a few steps of the ladder and stopped in his tracks. He imagined the sewer water turning into a wave, and just as he was about to make the next move, he heard Martha's voice.

"Andy, you must focus on the imagery of a tidal wave above you. Go into a deep state and release."

"I got it," Andy said. He went quiet, seeing the water appear above him, and he pictured the four robots standing there, not expecting a surprise attack. With all his strength, he watched the waters gather around them and short-circuit them. At the count of three, he released this image with full concentration. He heard, water bubbling above them, and, within minutes, the sounds of sparks and distant ringing.

"We have five minutes to get out!" Wendy yelled.

"Has the alarm been sounded?" Zack asked.

"Yes, it has!" Wendy screamed.

John popped the sewer lid up with super speed and the children climbed out and ran down the road. They could hear several wheels turning and approaching them from all sides.

"We must hurry," Wendy said. The children were super-fast to run into the door of the abandoned warehouse.

"That should be safe," Wendy said.

The streets of Old York looked uninviting.
Many buildings have been destroyed
and litter was everywhere.

The party hid behind factory boxes with the words "CORT Fruit Inc written on them."

They sat quietly behind the boxes, listening to the noises that sounded like bangs and whistles. Soon, the commotion outside stopped.

"It's all clear," Wendy said.

"Is that what you have seen?" Zack asked.

"Give me a minute, I will check." The boys watched as, once again, she closed her eyes and fell in a deep trance. Five minutes later, she looked at them.

"It is all clear," she confirmed.

The party got out from hiding and tried to be careful as they headed out. The place was dark and scary: animal carcasses were hanging on hooks, huge boxes were scattered everywhere, and the purple lights added mystery to this place.

"Is this where we are supposed face death?" Andy wondered.

"I do not think so," John stated.

"Do you know where?" Andy questioned.

"I can only think of one place that Martha meant," Wendy said.

"Where is it?" Andy called out.

"It has to be Grand Central,"

"How far is it?" Zack questioned. "Why do you think it is the place she meant?"

"An event took place there that caused a massive death for thousands," Wendy stated.

"What did they do with the station?" Andy asked.

"A horrible thing. They turned it into a museum

and hid a small headquarters on the bottom level," Wendy declared.

"Does it mean it will be hard to get to?" Andy wondered.

"It will be hard, but if we use our talents, we should be good," Wendy added.

"Let's go now," Andy called out.

"It will not be a good time now. We need to find a place to rest first," Wendy said.

They dashed out of the door. The party ran through the streets, but no one paid any attention to them. People moved in a straight line in both directions. The heroes tried to blend with the crowd. The rest of the way was quiet. They kept close to each other.

"Do not look at the television," Wendy reminded them.

"Do you have any of those cool glasses we were wearing before?" Zack questioned.

"I forgot them this time, so be careful," Wendy said.

The streets of Old York looked uninviting. Many buildings had been destroyed and garbage was everywhere. The stores were closed, and shattered glass covered the streets. Plywood covered the storefronts and people were scarce. The people they did see looked scared and worried. The party walked in complete silence. Old York was only a skeleton of New York City. Finally, they saw the old train station in front of them.

Chapter 8
Grand Central

"**W**e are here," John said.

"What next?" Wendy wondered.

"I believe we shouldn't enter until dark," Zack suggested.

"It is a good idea, Zack," Wendy said with a smile.

"Hey, John, do you know of any inn we can stay in until dark?" Andy asked.

"Wendy has the connections, not me," John answered.

"I might know of a place, but you need to give me twenty minutes to plan," Wendy responded.

"We will try to stay out of trouble," Zack said.

"You better. I do not want to lose anyone ever again," Wendy said. She hit Zack on the back and ran off. It made Zack feel liked and in charge.

"Okay, boys, where do we hide?" Zack asked.

"I think it is best to try to blend in," John added.

"How do we do that?" Andy asked.

"Watch and learn. All it takes is a little acting," John started to move like a robot. His feet moved slowly, while he was pacing back and forth. It was amazing how his whole body changed. It took Zack and Andy a few minutes as well, but it became a game and a competition for the boys. The brothers tried to be as good as John, but they couldn't.

The game made the twenty minutes go fast and, before they knew it, Wendy was back.

"I set all the plans. Now, stop playing around and come," she commanded.

"I hope this place has a shower," Andy said.

"Yes, I feel like a sewage pipe," Zack complained.

"I think we all do," John said. They followed Wendy. The trip itself was no longer than fifteen minutes. Soon, they arrived at a storefront. The door itself was solid brick. Wendy took out her keychain and touched the right side of the door. This motion caused a keyhole to appear. She put the key in and turned it, and a door swung open. They entered a large stairway that led them underground. The moment they took the first step down, the door slammed shut.

"We should be safe here. The leader, Robert, will take care of us and assist us in finding Grand Central later."

"Why is Grand Central the place where we will face death?" Andy wondered.

"You will find out soon enough," Wendy asserted.

The heroes went down the stairs quietly until they found themselves in front of an entrance to an old train tunnel. After they passed through the entrance, a rather tall man greeted them. He had long blond hair and green eyes. He was wearing a green and black uniform made from something that looked like leather. It fit very tightly around his body.

"Hello, Zack, Andy, John, and Wendy. Welcome to the New York Underground," Robert stated. His voice seemed to be low and shaky. He looked as if he was nervous about everything.

"Nice to meet you," Zack said.

"A pleasure," Andy added.

"What's up, man?" John said.

Robert ran up to John and picked him up. "I thought we had lost you!"

"You almost did, but thanks to Wendy and Andy, my head was not turned to mush."

"I guess this is where you are from," Andy wondered.

"Yes, I was sent here about six years ago. My training took longer than usual," John added. The group marched through the tunnel completely trusting Robert.

"Where can we take a shower?" Zack asked.

"Yeah, I am sick of this smell," Andy hinted.

"There is a shower machine that cleans and massages your bodies. I think you will like it," John said.

Zack looked at John with a smile.

"Yes, let me show you where it is," Robert pointed to the right.

"I will take them," John insisted.

He ran off with happiness. Wendy and the boys followed him. They soon approached a large chamber. In large letters, it said, "The Showers." Near the chamber were four latex one-piece suits, towels, and chairs.

"Here we are," John said as he peeled off his

clothing, stood nude for a moment, and walked in. Andy was next, followed by Wendy and Zack. The four kids fit perfectly in the chamber. The moment they walked in, brushes cleaned them, washing all their body parts from head to toe. By now, the boys were used to all these coed showers.

The brushes scraped them with a foam-like substance. Water poured over them and finally some kind of machine scanned them. The four nude kids came back out and put on the fresh clothing left for them. The suits fit perfectly over their bodies. They felt unbelievably soft and comfortable as well.

After everyone was dressed and cleaned, Andy said, "That was so cool and felt great."

"Yes, it was. I feel like new now," Zack added.

"Did I tell you the machine was invented by our old founders?" John asked.

"There are rumors that, in the old days, the showers were used for cars," Wendy said.

"I can tell you, in our world, that machine is called a car wash," Zack said.

"It washed cars, but not people," Andy added.

"What did they do in the end?" Zack questioned.

"I will show you. It is kind of cool," John said. He took them over to printer nearby. It was beeping and zipping. Four huge papers came out from the bottom.

"We call this a scanner," John said. "It shows the details of the human body."

It was fully colored and showed layers of each kid: upper, middle, and deep. The first layer showed everyone's skin and full body; the middle layer showed the detail of the muscles, joints, and tendons. The deep layer showed all the organs and bones.

"I had no idea what I looked like on the inside," Zack said.

"Why were we scanned?" Andy wondered.

"It is to make sure that the visitors have no robot parts or chips inside them," John said.

"Yep, and all four of us are clean. We are still human," Wendy said.

"I understand," Andy said.

"Now is the best part," John said.

"Yes, mealtime!" Wendy added.

The boys had forgotten how hungry they were. They followed Wendy down the hall and entered a large room. It was the meal room back in the underground where the walls had the resistance's colors on them.

Several large oak tables were set with the finest foods. Many of them were already full of people and goodies. Most of the individuals were children with a few adults, and seniors as well. Four seats were left open for the party. Robert was sitting in the center, and around him were others—most likely his ranked officers. The four empty seats were near Robert. Right when the children were about to sit, they heard a bell ring.

"Attention, brothers and sisters, we have very special guests with us, and we will be celebrating them this afternoon!" Robert declared.

Zack could not believe how loud Robert's voice

was. After Robert spoke, the room filled with cheers and claps. Zack looked out at the large room and watched as everyone stood up. There must have been at least 250 people all dressed in the same uniform.

"Please welcome our brothers John, Zack, and Andy, and our sister Wendy. Please stand honored guests." Robert pointed at them. The four children moved to the front of the stage and faced the huge crowd. It felt like they were part of a show.

Andy, once again, heard Martha's voice in his head: "My boy, the time has come. You have to sneak away."

"Wouldn't that be noticed?" Andy wondered.

"I will make sure it is not. Now, get going and follow my voice," Martha continued.

"Okay, here I go." Andy started running off the stage. It felt like he had turned invisible. As he was running away, the voices faded.

"Andy, use the central door," Martha instructed.

Andy let his gut lead him. He knew his destination was Grand Central. After he left through the main door, he found himself back in a huge tunnel. It must have been at least twenty feet high. It reminded him of the high ceilings he once saw inside The New York Public Library. Soon, he saw a sign that read 34th Street. The writing was very worn out, but he was able to make out the numbers.

"You are almost there," Martha stated.

"Yes, please guide me where to go," Andy pleaded.

"Go to the left tunnel and get your gift ready. You will encounter robots soon."

Andy left through the main door and found himself
back inside a huge tunnel. It must have been
at least twenty feet high.

"Okay. Martha, I am very scared."

"It will be all good. Now, go!"

Andy felt like he lost control of his body for a moment. Then, his control came back. He ran through the tunnel and entered darkness. He could sense that fast trains traveled through these tunnels once. Just thinking about that, he felt his whole-body shake. Andy picked up speed and he came out into Grand Central Station. Five robots were waiting to attack him.

"Identify yourself!" a harsh voice called out.

Andy said nothing and started to focus on the spot where the robots stood.

"I will count to five. If you do not talk, I will arrest you."

"I am Andy, son of Adam, and am here to destroy you," Andy declared.

"Isn't he a cute one?" another robotic voice said.

"I think I will make him my personal slave," said another.

Once again, Andy focused on the area where the robots were standing and, suddenly, a huge hole swallowed all the robots together. He could hear the shattering of iron and the sparking of live wires. Andy jumped back and felt an energy rush run through his whole body.

"You are amazing, my boy," Martha's voice sounded.

"What did I just do?" Andy asked.

"You are beginning to develop your mental power.

When you can control elements, this power can be manifested in many ways."

"I had no idea I had it in me."

"You have much more power than you know, Andy."

"Where do I go now?"

"Now you must face death and, once you do that, you will find The Mirror Rod."

"Do you mean my own death?" Andy asked with fear on his face.

"You will know soon enough. Now, go up the stairs."

"Yes, Martha."

Taking a few deep breaths, Andy started to move up quietly. He could see a red light above. Once he got closer, he felt a burning heat go through his body. It felt much hotter than anything he ever felt before.

"Keep on moving up. Your cool suit should kick in shortly," Martha's voice echoed in his head.

"Yes, Martha, I am going as fast as I can," Andy said.

After he climbed up about fifteen steps, he was ready to strip because his body felt steaming hot. When he placed his hand on his suit to remove it, a deep, cool feeling stopped him. Martha was right: his suit felt like ice. It balanced out everything. Before he knew it, he found himself upstairs.

He remembered the old Grand Central Station; he had gone through it many times. The last time he was here was on Christmas Eve. Small shops lined the walls. People were rushing to buy last-minute gifts. The sweet smell of cocoa and freshly baked goods filled the air.

What he saw now made his heart stop and made him cry. Instead of beautiful shops, there were glass cases lined against the walls. Frozen human bodies were behind them. Some people were dead, and others just seemed to be sleeping. Grand Central looked like a storage facility for human flesh.

"Welcome to what CORT calls The Human Factory," Martha whispered. "Some are used for food, others are used for science, and others are turned into half-bots."

"It is outrageous," Andy murmured.

"CORT is very cruel."

"How do I face death?"

"Look around. You'll find out." Martha's voice faded away.

Andy knew he had a mission. He noticed that each case had basic information on it. In front of him was the body of a seventeen-year-old girl, and to the left he noticed a twenty-four-year-old man. On the right, he saw a seven-year-old boy, and a bit further was a fifteen-year-old girl. Each of them seemed to be frozen in time. Fifty feet in front of him, Andy noticed a dead man. In his hands, he was holding a strange glass rod. A strong smell of rotting flesh filled Andy's nose. It was the first time Andy faced death.

When the boy grabbed for the rod, he heard a flying dart coming from somewhere. He ducked down as it whizzed by his head and hit a glass case. He saw another dart coming toward him. Andy flipped over, landing on his feet. When he was just about to lose his balance, another dart went through his legs. The lad felt like a gymnast. He was surprised at his agility. Just as he took the rod, a fourth dart hit his leg. He felt a harsh pain flow through his body and then he fainted. He woke up to the sound of loud footsteps. He was next to the man, and in front of him was the body of a young woman. The dart must have broken a case. He looked at his foot, which was turning brown. The dart must have been poisoned. His eyes were about to close, but he used all his strength to keep awake. An idea came to him. He had the ability to control elements, and he learned in school that the human body was like 98 percent water. Before he closed his eyes, he just caught a wink of two robots coming toward him. He remembered what Martha had taught him: to look within and create the magic.

The emotions and memories of his childhood home followed. He felt the love of his family; he saw his dog and the baseball games he won. He heard the song his mom sang to him before bedtime. He remembered how his friends and family used to gather for various holidays and all the fun they used to have. A powerful burst of energy filled his body. He focused on how his leg felt before the dart hit. Using his mind, he saw his injured leg healing and blood flowing through it. The rod in his hands started to glow. When the robots were about to grab him, Andy vanished and the room he was in did too. Andy saw a tunnel of rainbow light, and his short life flashed in front of him. Before he realized it, he had landed back at the 34th Street station. He opened his eyes, and saw Zack, Wendy, John, and Robert standing in front of him.

"You did it," Martha's voice said and once again vanished.

"Amazing, Andy. You are the first one in decades who has such powerful magic," Wendy praised him.

"You are the king," John added.

"I am proud of you, little bro," Zack said.

Andy looked around the old station, and realized his suit was tattered. All that was left on his leg was a small red dot where the dart hit. At that moment, he smiled at everyone and fainted from exhaustion.

Chapter 9
Awakening Hope

A ndy woke up thirty minutes later in the hospital wing. He felt much better. Wendy, Robert, Zack, John, and Joy were looking at him.

"Welcome back, super boy," Wendy smiled.

"Hey, guys," Andy said, still feeling sleepy.

"I see you found the first item," Wendy stated.

"Did I do everything right?" Andy questioned.

"We were supposed to go together. Things turned out different," Wendy replied.

"I am happy you are safe," Zack added as he hugged Andy.

"You gave our crew lots of work by bringing back all those people," Robert said.

"Can you help them?" Andy wondered.

"As a matter of fact, we can, but we decided to wait until you woke up."

"I cannot wait to show you our amazing machine," John screamed with excitement.

"You saved many people today from CORT's claws," Robert added.

"How many people did I bring with me?" Andy wondered.

"We counted about a hundred and fifty," Robert said.

"I wish I could have brought more."

"Andy, you used powerful magic. How did you learn it?" Wendy questioned.

"I have no idea. It just happened at that moment."

"It means you have hidden gifts yet to be discovered!"

"I believe that by using Wonder Woods to get to Icy City, you can develop those talents," John called out.

"I heard those woods can be very dangerous to move through," Wendy said.

"Do not worry, guys, I will help you. But for now, let's unfreeze those people," Robert addressed the party.

Feeling better and recovering from the powerful magic, Andy followed John, Wendy, and Zack over to 34th Street station. The site remained the same. The party was met by thirty people dressed in one-piece suits.

"These people will help you out like I will," John explained.

"I am with you too, bro," Zack added.

"Me too," Wendy added.

"What do we do, John?" Andy questioned.

John went over to a corner of the station and brought back a large hammer and a rod. Andy noticed that the rod in John's hands looked like the first weapon he got from Wendy.

"I had no idea it could be used that way," Andy said.

"I see you recognize the item," John stated.

"Yes, I certainly do."

"Do you remember how it sparks and has the ability to destroy robots?".

"Yes, I remember."

"It also raises people from the dead," John explained.

Andy looked in amazement as John turned the rod over. In the other hand, he held the hammer. He walked over to one of the cases and smashed it open. The glass cracked easily, and a body fell out. It was a thirteen-year-old girl. John placed the rod on the girl's heart; then the rod emitted a white spark, and, within seconds, she woke up.

"That is known as the spark of life," John called out.

The girl smiled and hugged John. After the hug, she walked toward the machine that scanned the party when they first got there.

"It looks easy enough," Andy said.

"I agree. Let's get to work," Zack added.

Andy looked at the other people in front of him. He walked over to where the items were and picked up a hammer and rod.

"Let's do this, friend!" Andy called out, raising the hammer and rod above his head. A big "Ho!" came from the small group of people, and soon, everyone got to work. The sound of cracking glass and the spark of life filled Penn Station.

A feeling of pure happiness and joy filled Andy's heart. He had a job to do, and he knew that millions of lost people had hope in the resistance. Out there, suffering was everywhere, but here, underground in a place that once was alive, that hope was getting stronger. A spark of love filled the station. The memories of the holiday season that Andy once had were flowing back. He understood that his inner magic was a powerful one and that one day after his mission ended, he would bring his brother and himself back home.

The whole process took about three hours. Overall, Andy saved sixteen people.

With each person he gave life to, he felt this deeper power grow. Things were starting to make sense. The power was starting to awaken inside. It revolved around human emotions: love, joy, and hope. As each of the puzzle pieces connected, Andy would develop new abilities. After all the work, Andy was incredibly tired and happy, but they would be spending one more night with the New York resistance. Before he fell asleep, Andy went over everything he had learned and all that had happened to him.

Chapter 10
Train Trip

In the morning, a loud knock woke Andy up. "Time for our meeting!" Wendy's cheerful voice called.

"I will be there soon," Andy answered.

"We will be meeting in the cafeteria," Wendy said as her footsteps faded away.

Andy's room was amazingly comfortable. The walls were covered by magazine cut-outs of superheroes long gone. He thought of his huge comic book collection left behind. He hoped that no one touched it.

He grabbed the mirror rod and his weapon. Before leaving the room, he took one last look at the images. He knew that one day he would be back there again. Taking a deep breath, he grabbed his backpack and stepped out. He noticed that the place was much more crowded. It occurred to him that many more people had been added to the resistance.

Yesterday, it was hard for Andy to process everything he did, but after a good sleep, it all made sense to him. As he walked down the hall, many individuals waved and smiled. Some of the people he did not recognize, but to be polite he waved back.

Andy got to the cafeteria just in time. He was happy to see everyone.

"Hello, sleepy head," Zack said.

"I have been up since 6:30 a.m.," John boasted.

Andy smiled at his friends and looked up at the clock. In large red floating numbers, it said 9 a.m.

"Okay now, let's get to business," Robert said.

"Robert's scouts have discovered some important information," Wendy said.

"Stop holding back, Wendy," John said.

"We have learned where the wonder stone is located," she acknowledged.

"What is it, anyway?" Andy wondered.

"It is rumored to be one of the three items belonging to the sages," John replied.

"The first one is that rod you found," Wendy said.

"Wow, I had no idea," Andy stated.

"How many of these items exist?" Zack inquired.

"According to legends, there are three," Wendy explained.

"What happens after all three are found?"

"It has never been done by anyone, so we do not know," Robert said.

"I guess we will find out soon enough," Andy said.

"It will be a tough journey," Wendy admitted.

"Yep, we are in it till the end," Andy said.

"Same here," John added.

"We all have been through so much, and we have a quest to do," Wendy stated.

"I will not be able to help you much, but I can give you one of these." Robert took out a red stone.

"Wow, is that the fire stone?" John asked.

"No, just an exploding stone. The firestone is hard to find. The Wonder Woods start just to the east of Wind Lake," Robert told.

"I know. We must take the train to Wind Lake and walk east," John said.

"Good luck, guys. We are all counting on you," Robert said.

"Please take care of the saved," Andy reminded him.

"We will. Stop by here on your way back." Robert went up to everybody and hugged them.

An hour later, the group was on the train. It reminded Zack of an old subway car. The only difference was it was a free ride. The signs of the lost civilization were everywhere. The brothers even noticed an old Coke advertisement. Half of it was ripped off, all that was left was a picture of a Coke can. Zack would have loved to have a soda now. He had not had one in a while. Another ad was from Camel brand smokes with the word "smooth" still written on it. They even noticed a JetBlue ad still intact.

The train traveled fast and, before the party could adjust, it came to an abrupt stop.

The voice announced, "Welcome to the Wind Lake."

When they stepped out, in the distance, they noticed a large lake surrounded by trees swinging back and forth.

"Do the Wonder Woods start here?" Andy questioned.

"They are about a mile away," Wendy said.

"We must be watchful because we will pass at least one Remake School," John warned.

"Maybe two. We must be ready for incoming attacks," Wendy added.

"Great, more danger. Nothing new," Zack said sarcastically.

Suddenly, Martha's voice sounded. "Andy, my dear, you can bypass the schools through a wind tunnel."

"How do I do this?"

"Use your elemental power control and focus on the Wind Lake," her voice called and disappeared.

"I have an idea," Andy told everyone telepathically.

"What is that?" John asked.

"How about bypassing the schools?"

"Can you hold us together?" Wendy wondered.

"I think I can. If I can transport half of a room, four kids should not be a problem," Andy insisted.

"Okay, go for it," Wendy encouraged him.

Everyone watched as Andy closed his eyes and went into deep thought.

He focused on the lake nearby, and the emotions followed. Andy thought back to the time his family celebrated his tenth birthday. They went to a huge bowling alley; it was full of amazing arcade games. That moment brought a huge smile to Andy's face. At that time, everyone felt the wind getting stronger. The four children were lifted from the station and they flew through the clouds over two small buildings. The scenery below flashed and zipped, and they landed. In front of them was a massive forest. It seemed to go on forever.

"Is this it?" Andy looked around.

"Wow, that was awesome," John exclaimed.

"Your power is great," Wendy praised him.

"Andy make sure our landing less painful next time," Zack complained.

"We are here," John declared.

"Do any of you know how to get through here?" Zack wondered.

"I have only been here once, and the path changes each time you visit," Wendy said.

"I grew up in Icy City," John said.

"Can you get us there?" Andy asked.

"I can try to guide you, but be warned, lots of dangers lurk everywhere."

"It means we all will have to work as one," Wendy said.

"Haven't we been doing that the whole time?" Andy added. They stood in front of the entrance, ready to embrace the unknown.

Chapter 11
Wonder Woods

The first five minutes were easy: it was just a red dirt road. Then strange things started to happen. Trees swayed and winds hit the group in the face. The forest started to thicken, and the light was turning into darkness.

"Now it is time to put on those masks," Wendy ordered.

Right away, the party put on their masks. No one complained. John moved freely and he knew the way. The children followed him closely. Zack observed the journey. There were so many turns and crossroads. As they got deeper, the temperature went up. The place started to look like a jungle. Exotic animals hung from trees; long snakes curled below the party's feet.

"We have to stop now," John said.

"Why is that?" Zack wondered.

"It is getting dark now," Wendy said.

"How can you tell this?" Andy asked.

"I can see the darkness just beyond that tree," Wendy replied.

"It is not safe to travel after dark here: too many dangers lurk in the night," John added.

"Are you sure that it is not an illusion?" Zack questioned.

"Give me a moment, guys, I will tell you," Andy insisted.

He sat nearby on something that looked like a stone. He was about to try to connect to Martha, but suddenly, he felt the stone shift under him.

"Hey, what's up with that?" Andy watched as the stone rolled away and he landed on the dirt.

The children could not resist laughing.

"What was that thing?" Andy asked.

"It is called a chair turtle. It is a very playful animal unless you are near a nest. If that was the case, you would probably get your head snapped off," John said.

"What other strange creatures lurk here?" Andy wondered.

"There are many that our people have studied, and many that are still unknown," John said.

"I still need a moment," Andy said. Everyone went quiet as Andy closed his eyes and called out to Martha. Not one single word was heard. He tried again and still silence.

"I can't access one of my gifts. It feels very strange," Andy said. He tried telepathically connecting to his brother Zack, but nothing happened. Andy opened his eyes and looked at his mates' faces.

"What happened?" Zack asked. "You look like a zombie."

Strange statements he never expected from his friends followed. Andy was about to scream out, but his instinct told him that something was up. His eyes started to water and things around him began to glow a vivid green light. The voices faded in the background.

"Catch that ball, boy," a voice called. Images swirled around him.

Memories of Remake Academy, the huge steel hands grabbing him, and the time he fell into the portal catching a ball. Everything spun into one large pot of stew. All the bad things people said, the times he got in trouble, and the moment he was surrounded by frozen bodies in Grand Central. The fears and the hopes and his adventures too. Andy's whole life was flashing in front of him. It was like a slideshow moving in cycles. The torture he had gone through and the time he spent with the resistance.

Somewhere far away, a familiar voice was screaming, "Wake up, little bro! Please come back to us." Andy's little body started to shake; he felt pain from head to toe. This feeling was more painful than torture.

"What is going on with him?" Zack asked.

"I have a feeling that the mirror rod has been activated," John said.

"What is that?"

"From the legends I have heard from my ancestors, the rod takes you to your inner self and brings out your worst fears and best hopes," Wendy said.

"Can you do anything?" Zack shouted.

"The best way is to wait," John suggested.

"I can't see my little brother suffer. I must help him."

"It will make things worse, believe me," Wendy said.

Zack felt his body pulled away from his brother by John, who said, "It is for the best."

Zack tried to fight John's grip, but the power was excessively strong for him, so he fainted into John's hands.

"We must wait this out," Wendy added.

"I know. Let us relax and sit down." John took something out of his bag. It was the size of a wallet. He threw it to the ground and a large blanket appeared.

"No way, John. It is a rare item," Wendy said. Then they picked Zack and Andy up and gently placed them nearby.

"I know. I kind of borrowed it back in Eastview," John said, smiling.

The two children sat quietly waiting for the two brothers to wake up.

Andy felt his body heat up and a vision of Ms. Weed 2 appeared again. Harsh words echoed around him: "There is no privacy here." Ms. Weed looked vastly different from before. She was a woman without any robot parts.

"Free me from this misery I live in," she cried out.

Andy could not believe what he heard. The woman tortured him, abused him, and embarrassed him. Now she was asking him to let her free. He could not understand anything.

A familiar distant voice called out to him: "Andy, my boy, to discover yourself and break the rod's spell, you must forgive your enemies." It was Martha's voice.

**The green light started to glow brighter,
and Andy noticed six strange yellow sparks
dancing around in a triangle.**

"I can't forgive Ms. Weed 2."

"You must have it in your heart to do so, as she is trapped too."

"But all the things she did to me..."

"She did not do them. CORT forced her. At one time, she was well respected and loved. She fell under CORT's spell."

"Who was she before?"

"She was a sage like you and me."

"I am no sage. I am nothing," Andy said with tears filling his eyes.

"Andy, you are powerful sage, and you have to believe in yourself. Look at all you have done," Martha reminded him.

The green light started to glow brighter, and Andy noticed six strange yellow sparks dancing around in a triangle.

"Those are so beautiful," he said.

"Yes, my boy, they are. The sixth one is you in the future. We will remake this world again."

"Which one is Ms. Weed?"

"She is number three, known as Zoey."

Andy could not believe her words. He had to do something. He made a promise to them. This was his chance.

"Zoey, I forgive you for what you did and with my love, I release you from bondage of CORT." Andy's voice echoed around him and that third spark flashed three times and vanished.

"You have done it," a voice in Andy's head echoed.

It was Zoey. "I am sorry for all that my counterpart did to you and the children. I will help you." The sparks disappeared, and Andy found himself next to Wendy, John, and Zack, who was still asleep. "Hey, guys," he said. His friends hugged him tight.

Meanwhile, back in CORT headquarters, Ms. Weed 2 felt a powerful energy go through her body. She watched as the machine inside her evaporated.

"I am Zoey again!" she called out. The communication with CORT Central stopped. "I have a mission." With the snap of her fingers, she was gone. Red lights started flashing.

"Red alert! Danger," a robotic voice screamed.

Back in Wonder Woods, Zack finally woke up. He looked at his brother and smiled.

"What did I miss?"

"Nothing much, big brother. All you did is fall asleep," Andy said with a smile.

"I must have been exhausted," Zack said.

"Indeed, you were," John agreed.

"Everything is clear," Wendy added.

The rest of the journey was quiet. Everyone was incredibly surprised at how easily John brought them to a massive door cut in the brick wall with the words "Icy City, where it all began" engraved on it.

"We are here," John said.

"How do we get in?" Zack asked.

"Let me take care of that." Wendy placed her hand just below the sign.

"Welcome home, Miss Wendy," a voice said, and

the massive door swung open. Behind the door stood a small man with a bald head.

"Come in, friends," he said. The four children entered, and the door slammed behind them. "You can remove the masks."

"George, you have not aged one year," John said. The man's face filled with a smile.

"You have aged many years, Mister John."

"I was tortured and humiliated, that is probably why," John said.

Soon all the masks were removed. It felt great to breathe fresh air again. The little man brought out a weird machine that looked like a metal detector. He scanned it over each of the kid's bodies.

"You guys are all clear. Welcome, Mister John, Mister Zack, Mister Andy, and Miss Wendy," he said.

"What was that thing?" Zack asked.

"It works like the machine back in Old York. It scans for robot chips, parts, and implants," Wendy said.

"They have to make sure no CORT officials were spying on us," John explained. After the scan, the party entered Icy City.

Chapter 12
Icy City

When the children entered Icy City, Zack saw piles of snow everywhere. People were dressed in simple colored suits that tightly hugged their bodies. The colors Zack noticed were green, red, blue, orange, black, and white. It must have been a class system. The roads were clean and were made of limestone and red dirt. Vendors were everywhere. The buildings were mostly gray and white. All the stores had glass windows and marble doorways. For a city that was full of piles of snow, the weather seemed perfectly balanced between cold and hot. The weather must have been artificially controlled. It reminded Zack of early spring weather in Trinity, New York. Even the smells reminded Zack of home.

As they walked down the streets, people waved and smiled at them. Zack wondered why the citizens were so happy here. He noticed that the children here were all less than four years old.

"How can everyone be so happy here when their own kids are fighting outside or are being brainwashed?" Zack wondered.

"For the citizens, it is actually an honor if their children are chosen to fight," John explained.

"Do you mean not all children are sent out to war?" Andy asked.

"No, about four out of ten are chosen," Wendy added.

"How come we cannot see any children in the street?" Zack asked.

"The ones who are not chosen usually work underground and get the worst jobs available," John declared.

"What kind of jobs?"

"Jobs included are cleaning sewage pipes, working in the mines, and others," John replied.

"In Trinity, that is illegal."

"Is it really so shameful not to be chosen?" Andy queried.

"Here, it is. It has been like that since the beginning of the civil war," Wendy said.

"How are individuals chosen?" Zack asked.

"Four times a year, everyone who turns five is tested in the arena," Wendy continued.

"The chosen ones are sent for one year of training to the temple of Elders and the others are given jobs," John said.

"Some kids get so upset that they escape to join the resistance," Wendy replied.

"Many of those poor souls are caught by CORT and put in Remake schools."

"Wow, it is so different from our culture," Zack said.

"It is very sad as well," Andy added.

"I was one of the lucky ones to make it to the Old York resistance, and, as you know, on one of my missions I was caught," John said.

The party continued to walk in the street. Andy and Zack wondered what kinds of tests these children had to go through. They could not imagine five-year-olds in competition.

"Are these tests open to the public?" Andy asked.

"Yes, they are a part of the Icy City's lifestyle like baseball is in your culture," John stated.

"Will we be able to see one?" Zack wondered.

"Yes, we all have to," Wendy said.

"Did Martha tell you?" Andy questioned.

"Yep, she did."

"We are in luck." John pointed to a note on a nearby wall. "Next test: tomorrow noon. Make sure to be there at eleven," a large sign read.

"John, is there a nice hotel here?" Zack asked.

"I think we can stay in the Icy Inn," John responded.

"It is a very popular hotel," Wendy added.

"What kind of money is used here?" Andy asked.

"The same as in the underground," Wendy said.

"I guess it makes sense," Zack agreed.

"It is printed here in Icy City," John said.

"Each resistance division has their own banks to hold it," Wendy said.

"A total of twenty," John said.

They all continued down the street. After passing a place that reminded Zack and Andy of the Broadway district in New York City, they came to a building that towered twenty feet. Across the street they noticed a massive stadium. It probably could hold at least 100,000 people.

"Is that it?" Andy wondered as he pointed toward the structure.

"Yep, it is," John said.

"It is very exciting," Zack added.

The children checked into the inn. Wendy handed a few paper notes to the front desk.

"Excellent, Miss Wendy, you can have the suite," the voice said. She was handed two card keys.

"Thank you, sir." Wendy smiled back and started to move. Everyone followed her to the lift, where she placed one of the key cards into the slot and the elevator went up. The party exited into a small hallway. There was only one door at the end of the hallway. The other card key fit perfectly.

"Welcome to Icy luxury," Wendy pointed at the open door.

They found themselves in a massive room. It had four bedrooms, three bathrooms, a full kitchen. Andy had never stayed in such a wonderful room his whole life. It was a great treat. The ancient oak table stood in the center of the room. It was fully set with food.

"Today, we relax, and tomorrow, we go to the arena," Wendy said and plunged into a comfy sofa.

The meal was amazing: meats, drinks, breads, cheeses, vegetables, and all kinds of treats. A man in his thirties served them, keeping their plates and cups always full. After everyone was full, they dispersed into their rooms. Andy's room had a large TV, a queen-sized bed, a minibar, and a desk. This bedroom was wonderfully comfortable. Andy fell asleep to Martha's voice telling him, "You did well, lad. After you watch the event tomorrow, you must convince everyone to spend a week of training in the Temple of the Elders. It will be your biggest challenge ever." When the voice went silent, Andy fell into a deep sleep.

Chapter 13
The Public Test

Everyone woke up early and breakfast was all ready for them. It was a large spread that had everything a persons' desires. Before they left, they had to put on white suits.

"What does white mean in this class system?" Zack wondered.

"Snow white is nobility, and ivory white means guests," John answered.

"What does it mean?"

"It means we get special privileges."

"It is actually pretty cool," Wendy said. "Okay, boys, it is time to go to the stadium." They headed out at 10:30 and were met in the entrance by a tall, sturdy man wearing black.

"It is great to see you, Wendy." The man welcomed and hugged Wendy.

"Indeed, it is, Mel," Wendy said and introduced him to the others.

"I need to scan you all," Mel requested.

"We are ready. Stand in line, boys," Wendy commanded.

They listened to her directions and lined up. The same detecting machine was used. It made a beeping sound when it went over each body.

"Thank you, guys. You are clear," Mel said.

"Nice to see you," Wendy added. She entered the side door, and the party followed. They walked among a large group of parents and five-year-old children. Each child was wearing a gray suit and was holding weapons.

Zack could not believe his eyes as they passed by. "Are those the contestants?"

"Yep, one group of four," John said.

"Every five-year-old has to take the test," Wendy said.

"Only about thirty-three children will make it today," John added.

"How many are participating?" Zack asked.

"About 330 each time," John said.

"Wow, only ten percent moves on," Andy said.

"Yep, that is about right, plus or minus a few," Wendy concluded.

"What is tested?" Andy asked.

"Each child is tested in five areas," John took over. "They are fear, speed, magic, flexibility, and fighting skills."

"Isn't that considered child abuse?" Zack interrupted.

"Not in Icy City," John continued.

"These kids have intense training for three and a half years," Wendy added.

"Wow, they start at one and a half?"

"Yep, as soon as they learn to walk," John said.

Zack and Andy were excited and soon they went up to the front row of seats.

The whole area was enclosed by glass and the party sat in the four middle seats. Six people wearing snow white robes were sitting next to them. Zack knew they had to be the nobility class. They did not talk much but paid careful attention to the large field in front of them. Soon a bell rang twelve times and a loud voice announced: "Welcome, ladies and gentlemen, to our quarter games. These five-year-olds trained hard and are ready to be tested. Keep in mind only thirty to forty of them will make it to Icy Temple. Good luck to you all." The voice went quiet, and four areas of the stadium opened.

Each group was called by color: Gray, Black, White, and Blue. After each color was called, about 100 five-year-olds came out from one of the opened gates.

The voice came back. "Our kids will be tested in five areas. If they score ninety-five or higher in each area, they will be chosen. Let us begin the fear test."

"What happens next?" Zack questioned.

"How is fear tested or even known?" Andy wondered.

"When the families send in applications to the tests, they tell the judges their child's biggest fears, and those fears are played out in the field," Wendy replied.

"Have contestants been injured or killed in this test?" Andy asked.

"Yep. Everyone knows the risks and must sign releases that state whatever happens to their children, they cannot file any kind of lawsuits against the city, the committee, or the judges," John added.

"That is horrible," Andy called out.

"It has been Icy City's laws since the civil war started. If any of the children get hurt or die during the tests, the family are treated like heroes and get many extras," Wendy explained.

"Basically, every citizen is willing to sacrifice their own children for a cause?" Andy wondered.

"That is so different from our world," Zack added.

"On our earth, five-year-olds are still considered babies, and our families would never put kids in such danger," Andy said.

"I probably would never be able to live in a world like that," John said.

The party watched as the fear tests started. These competitions included everything from spiders and snakes to drowning and beyond. Some of the tests the boys saw would have scared them too, and they were much older. By the end of the first round, only 250 passed. Most of them ended up injured and some even died.

Now Andy understood, it all came down to survival. If you survived a test, you would get a score of ninety-five or more. As each test was announced and finished, the number of kids went down. The party saw some amazing things over the course of three hours. They witnessed magic that was much more powerful than Andy had ever known. As for speed, many of the kids were faster than John, who was the fastest in the underground. One five-year-old dug a forty-foot hole in two minutes. It was amazing to see all this played out in front of them. By the time, the fourth test came around, only 100 children were left to continue.

This was the first time ever that the brothers had seen such an amazing show. It was five times better than any sports game.

The final test arrived quickly. Eighty children were left.

"This one is my favorite," Wendy whispered.

"By showing fighting skills, the winners will be chosen," John added.

"Will those five-year-olds fight each other?" Zack asked.

"That is right. The winners of the fight will be sent to Icy Temple for one more year of training," Wendy said.

"After that, they will be sent out to various resistance groups throughout the kingdom," John said.

The voice came back again: "We started with four hundred children and now only eighty are left." The bell rang three more times, lights flashed, and the last eighty children came out wearing black or white.

Cheers filled the arena, and a battle began. All the five-year-olds had chosen a weapon of their liking. In front of them, a bloody battle was taking place. At some points, both Zack and Andy had to look away. This was no show, but a battle to the end. The children had to combine all skills to survive. After forty minutes, the White team remained standing. It was evenly divided with twenty boys and twenty girls. Massive cheers filled the stadium. As for the Black team, fifteen died on the battlefield and twenty-five were injured. Ten monks came in and took the forty winning children away.

"Will they see their families again?" Andy asked.

"Only after a year," John stated.

"They get a one-week visit with them before they are transferred to the resistance," Wendy said. "The ones who died will be honored, and the others will be given jobs in the city," John added.

"What kind of jobs are there?" Zack asked.

"The most common jobs they get are mines, underground takers, garbage clean-up, farmers, servants, or apprentices."

"Wow, very harsh."

"How many children have been lost to those tests over the years?" Andy asked.

"No one knows, but probably many thousands," John said.

"Keep in mind it is a great honor to be tested," Wendy added.

"I understand, but I do not get the logic behind it at all," Zack said.

"It is very tough for outsiders to understand, but it is also hard for me to understand your world too," Wendy said.

"Wendy and I both grew up here," John said.

"I get it. Now, what do we do next?" Andy asked.

"We will be spending a week in Icy Temple to get

trained and understand what the others go through," Wendy answered.

"That is so cool," Andy said, excited.

"I have already made the plans," Wendy said.

"When do we start?" Zack questioned.

"Tomorrow the monks will pick us up," Wendy said.

With those words, the party got off the seats and headed to the exit.

Chapter 14
Looking Deep

In the morning, all four children woke up early. After witnessing the deadly competition, they were upset.

"I still don't understand how families can sacrifice their own children," Andy wondered.

"Yeah, very strict rules," Zack added.

"You lads should not be surprised that much. You both sacrificed so much already," Wendy reminded them.

"We did not have much choice. The portal threw us both into the war," Zack said.

"No, Andy was taken by accident. You, as a big brother, had to save him," Wendy corrected.

"Of course, I had to. I could not let my family be sad," Zack said.

"In a way, your parents lost much as well," Wendy said.

"I do hope Mom and Dad are doing all right back home," Andy said.

"They will not know the difference once you learn to control the time portal," Wendy admitted.

"Really? How is that possible?"

"That you will learn in Icy Temple."

"If it is a time portal, does that mean I can land just before I vanish?" Andy said.

"No, you must not do that or your whole mission will be destroyed," Wendy said.

"When do I land?"

"I would guess it will have to be three hours after I leave," Zack suggested.

"Yes, that is the best time to land," Wendy agreed.

"It makes sense. Both of us will have an hour to get to dinner," Zack said.

"Smart idea," John added.

"That is what I will do," Andy promised.

"The sacrifices that you witnessed yesterday are something that our people are proud to do here so they can bring peace back," Wendy explained.

"Yes. It is the death of a few to save many," John added.

It was hard to accept, but it did make sense. Zack remembered how, back in history class, he was taught that in war, people suffer and die. It was part of a bigger plan for peace.

Soon they heard the somber music playing just outside the window.

"That is the hero ceremony for those kids who died yesterday," John said. "They are treated like heroes, and everyone, whatever the age, dreams of being a hero one day, even if in death."

The group prayed together in the room and cried for the fallen. Then they were off toward Icy Temple.

The trip was quiet, and it was interesting to see what kind of training was given to the children. They knew that they would learn to master their gifts and magic. The temple was standing on top of a hill. It was a round white structure with only a few windows.

Strangely enough, when they got closer, they saw it was surrounded by several gardens and green fields. Icy Temple was much larger than it seemed at first.

Right before they entered, Andy heard Martha's telepathic voice: "Andy, darling, after you train, you will find the second item. It is hidden deep in the temple. It will be a challenging test, but you must pass it."

"What am I looking for, anyway?" Andy wondered.

"It is a stone. Now, good luck, my boy." With those words, the voice faded and a knock on the door woke Andy up. A short man with a shaven head pushed the door open. The party entered the temple. It was dark inside, and the snoring of sleeping children filled the room.

"Why is everyone sleeping?" Wendy questioned.

"Welcome, Miss Wendy. It is afternoon nap time for the warriors," the bald man said.

It did make sense since the training must be very tough, and back in school, Zack learned about the importance of sleep.

"Miss Wendy, you will be able to meet the children in about two hours, and my brothers will explain your jobs."

"Thank you, Master Quincy." Wendy bowed to the master.

"For now, let brother Jim show you to your rooms. Please come back to the temple's center in about an hour and a half."

"Wonderful. Thanks, Master Quincy," Wendy said.

"Brother Jim is practicing silence for a week," Quincy explained.

The party bowed to Master Quincy and closely followed Jim to the back of the temple. Jim pointed at the four doors and walked away.

"I guess this is it," John said.

"Let's meet back here in an hour or so," Wendy suggested.

"Okay," the three boys said together and entered their rooms.

Andy found his room quite simple. There was a bed, a desk, a dresser, and a small bathroom. There was no radio or TV. Andy felt very tired, and he figured why not take a shower and relax a little. He went inside and found that the shower was already being used. He did not understand what was going on. It hit him there were two entrances and he understood that he was sharing it with one of his friends. He heard John's voice singing in the shower.

"Hey, hurry up," Andy called out.

"Okay, roomie, I will be done in fifteen minutes," John answered back and continued to sing. Andy took a big yawn and went back to his room. He sat at the desk.

"Andy," he heard a voice in his head. It was John's.

"What is it, man?" Andy asked telepathically.

"The water is cold, weird, and white," John said.

"What do you feel?" Andy called back.

"Very cold." With that, the connection was suddenly interrupted.

Andy ran right into the bathroom and found John's body on the floor. He was purple and shivering.

"What did you do?" Andy said.

"I have no idea. I think the monks want us dead," John whispered.

Andy picked John up, carried him into his room, and put him on his bed. He sent a telepathic message to Wendy and Zack.

Only Zack answered him back. "Wendy turned purple too."

"Brother bring her here. We can save them."

I still do not understand what is going on with these monks, Andy thought.

Five minutes later, a loud knock was heard at Andy's door. He ran over, opened it, and helped Zack bring in Wendy's body. "Should we call someone?"

"Are you mad? Two of our friends are almost dead!" Zack called out.

Wendy's and John's breathing was slight, but it still existed.

"Why do you think these people want us dead?" Andy asked.

"I will be right back. It might have been a mistake," Zack stated.

He went inside the bathroom and understood what happened. Cold water was still flowing and making a large ice pile in the bath. Zack turned the water off and discovered what went wrong. In large letters were three words written in 3D: freezing, warm, and boiling. John turned the faucet to frozen and got in. It was still odd why would there be a frozen setting.

Zack went back into the room and told Andy, "It was not the monks. Our friends cannot read."

"I found a switch on my bed," Andy replied.

He placed his hand to the word "warm," one of three words he saw. The other two read "hot" and "cool."

The moment he did this, the bed heated up and within two minutes, both Wendy and John started to turn pink again. They woke up five minutes later and looked at the brothers.

"What happened?" Wendy asked.

"You both almost froze to death," Andy explained.

"I am very sorry to scare you that much," Wendy apologized. She gave them both big hugs.

"Me too, dude," John said.

"You guys definitely did. Follow me and let me show you how the shower works," Zack insisted.

Wendy looked at John and Zack and did what he told her. The three of them made it back into the bathroom. They watched carefully as Zack turned the faucet to the center and right away warm water flowed.

"Really, man?" Zack said and walked out the room and Wendy followed. Zack smiled at her, because when her beautiful body stood next to him, he felt warmth all over. His face became bright red. Wendy swung her body back and forth a few times and gave Zack a large kiss and walked out of the room. Zack smiled and winked at Andy and left.

"I never understood teens," Andy said to himself. He sat down on his bed and listened to John's singing in the shower.

"Give me a break, man, your voice sounds like a dead sheep," Andy complained.

"You hurt my feelings, Andy." John got out of the shower, rolled up one of the towels, and smacked his friend.

"Ouch!" Andy screamed. He watched as John's body disappeared behind his door. He heard the door being locked from the other side.

"Finally, I have some peace," Andy said to himself as he locked the door of the bathroom side and removed all his clothing to take a shower. Andy took a deep breath, turned on the warm water, and finally got a chance to relax. After he dried off, he decided to practice his magic. He had about forty minutes before the meeting. He sat on his bed and opened his mind to that inner magic he used back in Grand Central. Right away, Andy felt inner peace and quiet. He concentrated on his past, focusing on the good times he used to have in camp. He remembered the campfires, the singing, and his friends. Suddenly, a vivid picture of a book appeared in his head. It was yellow, green, and orange. In bold red letters was written, "Book of Know Magic." The letters danced in circles, and then disappeared. Andy felt something hit his knees hard.

"Ouch!" he screamed. When he came from his inner thoughts, he discovered the book on his knees. Did he just materialize it, or did it come from a parallel world? He did not understand how or why.

Chapter 15
Book of Know

A ndy heard a loud knock on his door. He quickly threw the book under the bed and figured he would study it later.

"It is time to go," Wendy's voice called to him.

"Okay," Andy said happily. He did not realize how fast time went. He thought he was out fifteen minutes, but it was more than an hour. Andy came out dressed in a fresh white robe that was given to him.

"Did you rest, Andy?" Wendy asked.

"I did, thank you," Andy said.

Soon, John and Zack appeared, each one wearing the same white robe as Andy had on. Jim came a few minutes later. "Okay, let me show the work you will be doing," he said.

The party followed him. The first stop was a huge room filled with all kinds of ancient books.

"This is our library, and the books and floors need some major cleaning. Any volunteers?" Jim asked.

"I got it," Andy said. He figured it would be the perfect place to learn.

"Great. In that closet over there, you will find all the necessary supplies. You can work for an hour before the meeting starts."

"Wonderful." Andy smiled and headed over to the closet.

"Shall we go on?" Jim asked.

The other three looked over at Andy and moved on.

Wendy got a job in the kitchen, John ended up working in the armory polishing weapons, and Zack was assigned to dishwashing.

Andy found the library mysterious but comfortable. He had worked in his school library and learned how to take care of books well. Inside the closet, he found some rags and a special cleaning fluid. He was surprised that everything he needed was ready for him. Andy decided to practice a bit. He sat in a large armchair and closed his eyes. He took a moment to picture the cloths being dipped in the fluid and added a memory of a time his family went to New York to see a musical. He even remembered the name "Oliver." He opened his eyes and felt a new feeling of being aware of things going on around him but still being in a relaxed state. He watched as rags hit water and started moving around the library, cleaning every book and dust particle in the room. They moved in perfect harmony, like dance partners, and in just thirty minutes, everything was sparkling, and the weak dust smell disappeared in the background. The cloths went back inside the closet and the dance was over.

Andy did not notice that a man was watching him the whole time. He must have been the temple's librarian. Andy felt a bit surprised to see another person here.

"That was an amazing show, young man," the librarian said.

"Thanks," Andy said, being a bit shy in front of someone he never met.

"What is your name? I have only seen that kind of power once."

"My name is Andy."

"A pleasure to meet you. My name is Ron." He put out his hand. Andy grabbed it and gave it a friendly shake. Ron must have been in his seventies, but he had a grip of a young man.

"Do you remember that person's name?" Andy wondered.

"I do, but I promised never to reveal it to anyone," Ron said.

"Okay." Andy smiled. He tried to read the man's mind, but it did not work. Andy thought about it for a moment and wondered if he could trust Ron. He still needed some answers about The Book of Know. Maybe it was transported from this library.

Andy felt the urge to ask one question that would answer everything for him.

"Ron, are you missing any books?"

"Not that I know of; I keep the best records."

"Since I am a guest, can I also use the library?" Andy asked.

"Yes, I heard you will be staying with us for a few weeks. Will you be interested in getting a library card?"

"That would be great." Andy followed Ron to an ancient desk.

Ron handed him a piece of paper. "Here we are, young wizard."

Andy looked at the application. It had three simple questions: 1) What is your name?

2) How long will you stay? 3) What is your room number?

He answered the first two questions easily, but he had no idea what his room was.

"Sir, I do not know my room number," he said honestly.

"I will hold your paper here; you can tell me tomorrow," Ron replied.

A monk came inside to inspect the job Andy did. He had never seen a cleaner room.

"Wonderful," the monk praised the boy.

"Thanks. Do you happen to know my room number?" Andy wondered.

The monk gave him a strange look and said, "Time for the meeting. My master has sent me to get you."

Andy waved at Ron and followed the monk.

"See you tomorrow," Ron called out.

Andy followed the monk through several doors and hallways. The temple's halls had pictures of former monks hanging everywhere. Occasionally, he would notice a young child's picture.

Soon they arrived at the Main Hall. Andy's friends were already there. In front of them, about 200 children dressed in red robes were waiting passionately. He recognized some of the winners from the games among them.

Andy watched as rags hit water and started
moving around the library cleaning every book
and dust particle in the room .

Quincy stood in the middle of the group. "Welcome to our special guests. I see all of you did amazing work on your jobs today."

The party listened carefully.

"We welcome you to our home. The jobs you were given will be done for two hours each day. Each of you will have a mentor who will not only watch over you, but who will teach you," Quincy continued.

Later, each child stepped forward and said their name and age.

"You also will be helping the children during the day," Quincy addressed the heroes.

The party watched each child, and they could only imagine what each of them went through. No one understood how they could help these kids out, but it looked like it would be part of the job.

After everyone was introduced, the brothers heard a great word: "Mealtime." Once that word was uttered, everyone got into line and started heading west from the Main Hall. The amazing smells came from the kitchen. It felt like camp back home. They entered a massive dining hall where about 300 eating spots were set up. The tables were scattered around the room. Zack sat together with three monks and many children. Andy was sitting next to John, Wendy, and two monks.

Before the food was brought in, everyone did a prayer, a small meditation, and a few chants. Andy had never experienced such intense power.

After everyone finished, tons of food was brought

out: breads, potatoes, meats, vegetables, and some things that Andy had never tried before.

Everyone ate in silence. Andy was starting to understand why.

After the meal was finished, more chants and prayers followed, and the huge room emptied out. Andy had no time to speak to anyone. He was certain that tomorrow he would be meeting many new people.

"Andy, ready to go back?" John asked.

"I am tired," Andy said. He was amazed at how quickly his friend adjusted to the new place. He took him right back to the room. Andy also noticed how Zack and Wendy did not go home with them. Could this mean his older brother was dating her? He promised himself that he would find out the details tomorrow.

"Good night, man," John said.

"Good night, John," Andy said.

With those words, the boys went into their rooms. Once Andy entered, he felt deep excitement and found The Book of Know where he had left it.

He tried to open the first page, but the book did not move. It was sealed shut. What could Andy do? An idea came to him. It was a magic book, so only magic could open it. He felt very exhausted and decided he would find time to do it later. He fell asleep in his bed, dreamed of his past, and wondered about the future.

Chapter 16
Dark World

The next day, Andy woke up to a clock ringing. It was 6 a.m. This was the first time he woke up so early. He had been used to sleeping much longer. John was already singing in the shower.

John could not sing at all, but Andy was used to his voice. Soon the singing in the shower faded and Andy heard silence. It was about time. He was itching to get in the shower and to relax a bit. Andy walked in and saw the bathroom empty. John's door remained open. Something was wrong here.

He heard Martha's voice in his head: "Andy, you have rescued one of the sages. Now is the time to rescue number two."

"Where is he trapped?" Andy asked.

"He is a part of that book that you have transported."

"What is his name?"

"His name is David."

"What must I do?"

"You must solve the word puzzle. When it is done, he will be let free. It takes great thinking. The magic that binds him is evil and strong," Martha said.

"Does it mean I have to fight evil?" Andy wondered.

"Yes, good luck. I am transferring you to The Dark World," Martha said. Her voice was gone.

Now Andy had a mission. He did not want anyone

to see him. The bathroom disappeared and in front of him a dark door materialized with words written in blood: *Enter at your own risk*. A cold chill went through Andy's veins. He placed his hand on the doorknob and pushed. He found himself in darkness. He closed his eyes and pictured red lights appearing all around him.

Suddenly, the whole place was lit up. In front of him was red brick road. The lights flashed for a few minutes and stabilized. Andy heard voices calling out to him: "Save us all!" Andy's body was in deep pain. The road was sucking his soul out. He had to do something. Once again, he closed his eyes and pictured his little body floating above the road. He added a strong memory of when he, his grandfather, and Zack went to a large fair. The strong sensation of happiness overtook him. He remembered smiling faces, the sweet smell of cotton candy, fried dough, and hot popcorn. He opened his eyes to find that he was floating above the red road. The draining stopped. He looked down below and saw death everywhere. He heard screams and cries for help. He knew he could not lose focus. Andy had an important job to do; if he failed, he would be gone forever.

Andy's concentration became stronger. He tried hard to ignore all the sounds around him. One mistake would make him fall and end it all. He noticed his red lights floating and lots of dead plants and trees everywhere. The smell reminded him of death itself.

Andy remembered about the breathing mask

he carried. He took it out and put it on. Now things started to get better. He floated slowly until he noticed a massive black and white castle. Andy's gut feeling told him that David would be trapped inside. Andy did not know what to expect, but he was ready for anything.

When Andy got there, he let his body fall slowly down. He found himself in a huge garden. It was full of all kinds of fruits and vegetables. His stomach was hurting, and his hunger was overwhelming. Deep inside, he knew that he should not eat anything, or he would be stuck.

Andy looked around and felt his body relax. He noticed a huge man in front of him.

"Welcome, young traveler," the man greeted the boy.

"Hello, sir," Andy said.

"I sense life in you. How can that be?"

"It is because I am alive."

"Only great wizards can cheat death," the man said.

"I guess that would be me," Andy replied with a smile.

The man gave off a large laugh that echoed in the garden. Andy's body shivered; it was like an earthquake. He could barely stand on his feet.

"You must be hungry, great wizard. Have some of my fruit."

"Thanks, sir, but I had a huge breakfast already."

"You must be hungry; your journey was so long," the man insisted again.

"I will be okay. I have come for one reason: to save David."

The man's eyes became bright red, and the fire was deep inside him.

"I am the keeper of Darkness, and I will destroy you," the man warned. Then in front of Andy's eyes, the man's clothing tore apart and he grew at least fifty feet tall. "Now you must die, lad!"

Andy jumped to the right as a ball of fire just passed near his head.

"Here we go!" Andy screamed. He once again felt his body float above the garden and land on the man's back. It felt great to be in control of his powers.

"Get off me now!" the man yelled.

Andy took his left hand and placed it on the man's large head. It felt so hot, but Andy fought on. He took a deep breath and pictured large ice balls. They appeared right away. Andy jumped to the side, and the ice balls turned into spikes and hit the giant. The first few melted, but the last five crushed the man's huge body. All that was left behind was a page from The Book of Know. It sizzled away and, in its place, appeared a very handsome man.

"You did well, great wizard," the newcomer praised.

"Thanks. You must be David," Andy said.

"Yes, I am. It's a pleasure. You helped me, and now I help you."

David gave Andy a light tap on his head which caused Andy to learn a new language.

**Andy opened his eyes and he found out
he was floating above The Red Brick Road.**

"Now, grab my robe, young wizard."

Andy did as he was told, and he felt peaceful moon energy fill his body. Before he knew it, he woke up on the floor of the bathroom and John's sour face was staring at him.

"Are you okay?" John wondered.

"I am great, thanks," Andy answered.

"Dude, you fainted and were out for twenty minutes."

"I needed to take care of something."

"You smell bad, man. Better take that shower," John recommended.

"I shall do that, but I need privacy," Andy said.

"Sure, I will be back in my room if you need me."

"Excellent." Andy watched as John left the bathroom and locked the door behind him. Just in case, he locked it on his side too. He removed all his clothing and got into the shower. It was great for him to finally relax. He had accomplished so much in his short life. He felt the warm water cover and clean his body. He dressed and went back inside his room.

The Book of Know opened easily in his hands, and he could understand each word clearly. No need for casting an open spell anymore. Andy wanted to try a few spells out but decided to hold back because he did not know what they could do. Who knows, maybe he could kill everyone off in the Icy Temple, or maybe he could transport the whole building to a dangerous world like he just came from? He decided it would be best for him to research this topic.

Andy heard a loud knock on his door. "Hey, Andy in room D13, come. We will be late."

It was Wendy.

Yes, he thought to himself, *I can get that library card*. "I am coming, Wendy!" After a few minutes, he came out. Andy made sure to hide the book very well, in a place where only he could find it. Today would be the perfect day for him to research the topic. Andy left the room quietly and bumped right into Wendy.

"Hey, watch it, lad," Wendy said with a smile.

"Right, shall we go? Do not forget I am only four years younger than you," Andy stated.

"That is why you are a lad."

Andy gave her a sad look.

Zack and John joined them a few minutes later.

"Did you know that Andy fainted today?" John asked.

"I told you, I am fine!" Andy screamed out.

"No need to raise your voice. I care about you, man," John said.

"I appreciate it. Thanks."

Andy soon was dropped off in the library.

"We will pick you up in two hours," Zack said, and the rest of the party left to their jobs. Andy was happy to get to work again.

"Young wizard," Ron greeted him.

"Hello, Ron."

"I sense you have been doing magic again; I can see it in your aura. And you got stronger."

"How do you know this?"

"Like you, I have a gift of sensing all kind of magic from others."

"Does everyone here in Icy Temple have powers?" Andy asked.

"Hell yeah. If you did not, you would never be able to live here," Ron said.

"How is that possible?"

"We feed from the temple, and the temple feeds from us."

"I get it. It is a joint effort."

"It is kind of like that, yes," Ron said.

"Oh, I almost forgot, I know my room number," Andy stated.

"That is wonderful. I will get you the application." Ron stepped behind the desk and brought back the paper.

Andy filled in "D13" and handed it back to Ron.

"Great job, young wizard." Ron went back to the desk and brought out a temporary card and handed it to Andy.

"Today you can clean out the back room. It has been catching dust for years," Ron ordered.

"I will do that. Can I research something after I finish the job?" Andy asked.

"Yes, you can. I will be working at my desk if you need me."

"Okay, I will. If I need help, I will find you." Andy walked to the back and used his magic again to clean everything up. He was done in forty minutes. It was amazing to see everything clean itself.

After he finished, Andy felt dizzy, and he fainted again. Everything went dark. He was just able to grab a chair the moment he fell.

Chapter 17
Wonder Stone

Ron jumped from his chair and ran like a deer to the back room. He found Andy unconscious on the floor.

"Oh, young man, you have so much to learn," he mumbled to himself. Ron took a wet cloth and wiped Andy's face with it. He placed his hand on Andy's chest. A deep blue ring of light came from it. He watched as the light wrapped around Andy's body. Soon his breathing came back, and Andy woke up.

"What happened to me?"

"Sit down young wizard. I must teach you something important about magic."

Andy looked up at the old wise monk with wide open eyes. He felt very tired. He sat down near a desk. Ron sat next to him and smiled.

"Young wizard, you must understand that sometimes you have to pay a price for magic." He raised one sleeve and showed Andy a rash that covered his whole arm. The skin looked horrible and it scared Andy. He wondered, could that be him one day?

"Thanks for sharing," Andy said. He learned that day to use magic only when necessary.

Twenty minutes later, Wendy stopped by to pick him up for training.

First, they had lunch, which was exceptionally

good. As usual, everything started with chants and prayers. After lunch, the party was taken to a massive field.

They observed as five- and six-year-olds trained. It was hard to believe that these children had skills like masters. The brothers were most impressed by the six-year-olds. The training included magic, fighting, flexibility, and speed.

Zack, Andy, John, and Wendy were placed into certain groups. Andy was placed in the magic group, Zack was placed in strength training, Wendy into flexibility, and John into speed.

All kinds of training were taking place. Each person moved as one. Andy was defeated in a magic contest by a few six-year-olds. He thought he was powerful, but how wrong he was. The training lasted for three hours.

One monk said, "Make magic a part of you." Andy connected to himself and went into a deep meditative state. He said a chant he remembered from The Book of Know. It rather sounded like "Invisibility." He mumbled to himself. He felt his body shake and in seconds, he vanished and was transported to a field. He decided to play around with the others, so he tapped Wendy on her leg. He pulled a fighting stick from a rack and threw it across the field. He giggled to himself. The moment he got out of that state, he appeared on the other side of the field.

One of the monks waved Andy over. Feeling a little tired, he came over to him.

"That magic is strong, and it is inside The Book of Know, which is supposed to be hidden deep in the tunnels under Old York. How did you learn that spell?" The monk's voice had a weird effect on Andy.

Without controlling himself, Andy said, "I brought that book to my room."

He turned red; he knew it was too late: everyone knew his secret now.

"You must put that book back right away. It was hidden there for an important reason. Every person who ever used its dark power died or went crazy and destroyed others," the monk said in a deep voice.

Once again, Andy lost control and instantly went into a deep state. He imagined The Book of Know disappearing from his room and being transported back to its hiding place. Andy had to do this; it did not belong to him.

The heavy training went on for a bit and Andy felt very tired. He was happy to hear the announcement that training was over, and it was time for dinner. The sun had set by now and everyone was called inside. They followed the same routine every day. The time flew by fast. In those two weeks, they attended one graduation ceremony. It was a great sight.

Thirty six-year-olds lined up on a huge stage. Everyone watched as they took off their training uniforms and handed them to the monks. In return they received the one-piece suits that Andy had seen back in Old York. The difference was the colors, which represented the resistance groups they were assigned to. After a feast, many hugs, smiles, and discussions, the children were put on a bus and taken to the center of Icy City. Andy was surprised how many resistance groups were in this world.

Wendy was so happy to see them. Each of the children went up to her and bowed down.

Wendy used her staff to knight each child and welcome them to her resistance.

A huge crowd had gathered, and Zack, Andy, John, and Wendy got front row seats.

It was hard to believe how cheerful everyone was. John and Zack knew what was waiting for these kids. The moment they went out into that world behind the walls, they could be killed at any moment or they could be captured and tortured by CORT.

The event was both sad and happy at the same time. It ended with a huge tunnel opening and the thirty children accompanied by a few monks leaving.

After the ceremony, the party went back to Icy Temple for the final night. A deep sadness overcame everyone, and the monks tried too hard to create a happy atmosphere.

When Andy came to his room, he looked back at all he had learned. He did feel a stronger link to himself, to people, and to nature. The monks taught him that if you could connect to the invisible, your magic would become stronger. When Andy was about to go to sleep, he again heard Martha's voice.

"Now is the time to find the wonder stone. You must use your mirror rod for this." After those words, the voice vanished, and Andy was alone again.

The rod was not too far from his bedside. Andy walked over and picked it up. He connected with everything he learned. The first connection was with him, the second connection was with nature, and the final connection was with the rod. As he stared into it, he felt himself being pulled in. He found himself in a glass greenhouse. It was full of all kinds of plants he had never seen in his life.

He focused his attention on everything around him. He was able to see colors over each plant. He noticed dark shades and light shades. Suddenly, he saw it: a huge pink crystal. He grabbed for it, but it moved away. He moved closer and tried to seize it and it moved once more.

Andy did not understand what to do. He tried transporting it toward him and could not. Out of nowhere, huge tree vines entangled Andy's feet. They were pulling him down. He tried to scream, but no sound came out. He let them pull him under. In his gut, he felt this was the right thing to do. Andy closed his eyes and gave in to the situation. He found himself in a crystal cave. His uniform was soaked, and he felt weak, but somehow, he managed to pull himself together.

He was facing a large rock head; it must have been wise and ancient. Andy tried hard not to lose his concentration.

"Welcome, young wizard," a deep voice said.

"Hello, Mr. Rock," Andy responded.

"You can call me Rocky for short."

"Rocky, nice to meet you."

"I have been expecting you. I guess you seek my stone."

"Can I please have it?"

"Only after you pass my test. I risk my stone and you risk your life."

"I am a bit young to die."

"That is the only way."

"What do you do, collect children's souls?" Andy wondered.

"Yes, something like that," Rocky said with an evil smile.

"I am ready."

"It is a riddle."

"How do I accept the challenge?"

"Put your hand on me, Andy."

"Okay." Andy placed his right hand on the rock head. The moment he touched it; a sharp pain went through him. "Ouch! How many children have you killed, anyway?"

"I do not kill children; I just take away their powers and make them a part of me."

"Like I said, you kill children. Now, tell me your riddle," Andy declared.

"I can't wait to make you a part of me. You are young and powerful," Rocky said with a wicked smile.

"Great, now stop chatting and give me your riddle!"

"I've never seen someone who is so excited to lose…"

"Enough already, Rocky!"

"Okay, young wizard, here is my riddle. It balances dark and light, but also lives inside us all."

"How many guesses do I get?" "

"One chance only."

"Okay, Rocky, you are talking about Gray Essence."

"Is that your final answer?"

"Yes, Gray Essence is my final answer."

"You are wise beyond your years, Andy. That is correct," Rocky said sadly.

The moment Rocky said those words, he vanished, and in his place, Andy saw a crystal stone. He took it and found himself back on his bed with the mirror rod and the wonder stone next to him. The Book of Know was long gone but that day, Andy learned that a person does not need a book to make magic.

Chapter 18
Dark Swamp

The next day, Wendy woke Andy up early with a loud bang on his door.

"Time to get out of here, Andy!"

"I am coming. What is the entire racket about?"

"I got us a lead. Now, let us go," Wendy rushed.

"What about breakfast?" Andy asked.

"It is packed to go."

"I will be ready in twenty."

"Okay."

He heard her go next door to John's room.

Andy put on his clothing, packed his backpack, and grabbed his weapons and new toys. Hunger was strong, but he could wait for a bit. Another journey would await them, but Andy did not really want to go anywhere. He was just adjusting to this new home.

Andy put all his strength together and stepped outside. Everyone from his party was waiting for him. Once again, they would journey.

"Where are we going?" he asked.

"Into the Dark Swamp, where the last part of our trip begins," Wendy explained.

"What is that place?" Zack asked.

"It is a very dangerous place," John added.

"Great, more fun," Zack said sarcastically.

"What kind of dangers will we face?" Andy wondered.

"We will find out," Wendy said.

As they approached the front door, all the monks and the remaining children were waiting for them.

The master monk was giving a farewell speech: "Thank you for helping us out. I hope you learned something."

"We did indeed," Wendy declared and thanked the monks.

After their goodbyes, the party was out the door. It was much colder outside by now and the city seemed less busy. Just to the east, the sun was about to rise.

Wendy was sure to get several extra layers of animal skins and food rations. When the party got closer to the gate, breakfast was served.

Andy could not believe this would probably be the last hot meal they would get in a while. They sat near the gate, ate, and watched the sunrise. With one last look at Icy City, they headed out.

The moment they exited the gate, the heat of the wasteland hit them in the face.

"Put your masks on, boys," Wendy commanded. "We are about to enter into a danger zone."

"Is the air different here than when we first entered Icy City?" Zack asked.

"You bet it is. It is best to wear those masks," Wendy said.

After several ooh's and ah's, the masks were put on. It was good to breathe normally; they could tell how dangerous it truly was outside. Only after about an hour of walking, the swampland started. It was scary to hear all the noises here. The hardest part was the darkness that slipped in suddenly.

Screams of strange creatures echoed around them, the temperature seemed to go up rapidly, and the stink of dead flesh was around. Out of nowhere, a creature that was half snake and half bull emerged. Its eyes glowed like coals and its nose hissed.

"Human flesh…have not had fresh meat in years," the creature yelled.

"Stand guard, guys," Wendy yelled out and took out the rod.

"I got this one," Andy said boldly. He took out the mirror rod with the wonder stone on it. He declared, in the strongest tone he could manage, "Look into your inner self, oh creature of darkness!"

Right at that moment, the rod started to glow like diamonds, and it emitted rainbow colors. The creature screamed out in pain and fell back.

"Wow, that is some powerful tool." John was impressed.

"That creature must have lots of darkness inside its lost soul," Wendy guessed.

"I kind of feel sad for it," Zack said.

"It would have eaten us alive," John reminded.

The instant the creature ran away, the rod went dark. Andy felt a large burn appear on his arm. "Ouch!"

"What just happened to my bro?" Zack asked.

"Wow, he has been marked by the sage mark," Wendy declared.

"What the hell is that?"

"It is the most powerful mark any person can get here, and it's very rare," John took over.

"Only five or six others in this whole world carry that mark," Wendy added.

Andy cried out in pain, and the mark glowed more.

"What can I do?" Zack asked, worried.

"Nothing right now. Your brother has been chosen to save others," Wendy said.

"I already rescued two sages," Andy said.

"Why did you not tell me this before?" Zack complained.

"All of us have our secrets, bro."

Soon, the mark glowed less, but it was still visible.

"Much better," Andy said.

"Let us stay behind Andy," Wendy suggested.

"He has more power than any of us combined," John added.

It did not surprise Zack much. His younger brother was always the popular one. He had many friends, many people were attracted to him.

Andy could not believe all that was happening to him at that moment. How could a mark appear from nowhere? So much weight was on his shoulders now. He had his friends, he had his brother, and just now he became a marked sage. When would it end?

The party continued walking through the dark swamp. No other creatures attacked or approached them. The rod led the way. It gave off a dazzling light that was much stronger than a flashlight. Suddenly, the darkness started to drift away. The party could not believe the true beauty spread in front of them.

"That is some powerful rod," John said.

"I had no idea that it had the power to bring light from darkness," Andy said, surprised.

"It is an amazing thing," Wendy said.

"In school, we were taught that combining three objects together will activate a powerful magic that only sages have the power to use," John added.

"Wait a moment, did you just say *three* parts?"

"Correct, Andy. They are the mirror rod, the wonder stone, and the dark shield," John said.

"Has the third item ever been found?"

"It is rumored to be guarded by two lost sages, somewhere deep in the swamp," Wendy concluded.

"Others say that it's a part of CORT Headquarters, but no one really knows," John added.

Soon, the light became much brighter and started dancing in circles around the party. It started as one blur that blinded the children, and then it grew and divided. Soon, faces appeared all around them.

"Hello, my young friends," Martha said.

"Martha, good to see you again," Wendy greeted.

"The pleasure is mine."

"Why did you not let us know that Andy would be so powerful?" Zack asked.

"It had to be held secret or massive death would have taken us all," Martha said.

"Can you tell us which rumor is true?" Andy asked.

"What are you talking about, my boy?"

"The last item—the dark shield—where is it found? Deep in the swamp or in CORT Central?"

"It is technically found in both places," Zoey said.

"How could that be?" Zack asked.

"CORT Central is deep in the Dark Swamp," Zoey said.

"You guys will need all three items. Your gifts and magic will destroy Spirral," Martha said.

"Is that thing very powerful?" Wendy asked.

"Yes, Miss Wendy, it truly is, and it is almost built," David said.

"I guess it means we are going to CORT Central next," John concluded.

"Yes, it will be there. Good luck, Children of Adam," Martha and the three sages vanished.

"Great, more fun for us," Zack said. The four heroes started walking through the forest. It was dark and scary. Fortunately, they didn't have to walk for a long time. Soon, they saw an enormous castle in front of them.

"We will do it," Wendy said. Once again, hope was shining. "This is it!" she screamed, pointing in front of her.

"We must be careful here," John added. The party moved toward CORT Central.

Chapter 19
CORT Central

CORT Central was a solid structure without windows or doors.

"How are we supposed to get in there?" Zack asked.

"Andy, it is up to you," Wendy said.

"You are the powerful one here," John added.

Andy did not know what to do. His mirror rod had stopped glowing, but a field of energy protected them from the creatures of the swamp. Andy thought hard. Then, an idea came to him. He remembered Ron's wise words: "Look deep inside." More words followed.

"Magic has consequences. Be careful."

"Stay back, my friends," Andy said in his best adult voice. He sat with his legs crossed in front of the building. The boy closed his eyes and tried to picture The Book of Know once again. He remembered a certain spell called "Knock." The rest of the party stepped a few feet back. Andy chanted the word "knock," and the rod started glowing again. Out of nowhere, the word Andy stated materialized in front of him. Everyone looked with amazement at this eleven-year-old boy. Zack wondered how his brother could be so powerful. Andy focused on that word and connected to it in a deeper state. It started dancing in semicircles around him, and finally went flying toward the brick structure. Once it hit, it vanished. Then Andy fell in Zack's arms.

Five minutes later, a sliding wall opened.

Zack and John had to bring Andy inside. The door shut behind them with a loud bang.

It took Andy ten minutes to wake up.

"Are you okay, man?" John asked with concern.

"I have no idea," Andy whispered.

"That was some powerful spell," Zack praised his brother.

"I feel very dizzy, but I was warned about controlling magic. Thank goodness for that."

"Whoever warned you probably saved your life," Wendy said.

"Yes, you used just enough power to open the gate briefly and you did not blast it open," John said.

"The perfect balance," Wendy said.

"Great, but I feel like tons of bricks fell on me," Andy said.

"You better save your energy and magic. We have a huge journey ahead," Wendy added.

"Yeah, little bro, we will do all the fighting now," Zack said.

"I am all in," John added.

"Make sure you can keep up with us," Wendy said.

"I will try my best!" Andy exclaimed.

The party was again moving. The trip through the company was a team effort. Andy did the least amount of work, but occasionally, he would destroy a robot or two. It was one huge maze full of dead ends and lurking danger. The party had to watch their step since the danger was both on the floor and all around them.

A few times, swords almost pinned them to a wall and huge holes swung open everywhere. They had to face several battles and had no time to rest at all.

Wendy had a chance to use her gift. She did a rather good job in guiding them through that large place.

They navigated the place for several hours. The gifts they were given had to be used carefully. John's hands were badly bruised.

Wendy's eyesight suffered too. As for Zack, every time he had to heal one of his friends, he would feel very dizzy. The heroes moved through narrow passages to avoid unpredictable surprises. They approached a solid iron door and heard buzzing and clicking sounds behind it.

"This has to be it," Wendy exclaimed.

"I feel so weak," John complained.

"I am tired," Andy said.

"We must not rest here," Zack encouraged.

"I agree, too much danger here," Wendy said.

Andy closed his eyes and connected to his inner self. First, he saw rainbows dashed in lights, followed by an image of a trip he and his family went on. It was a hot August day. The sun was shining, and they decided to hang out in Central Park. Father brought a Frisbee with them. It was his favorite day in his life. They did not usually spend so much time together on family trips. With work and school, time was limited.

**The children stayed close together
striking each robot as they attacked them.**

That day had been planned two weeks in advance. Out of nowhere, Andy heard Martha's voice.

"My boy, we are with you right now. We are starting to get back our power, and our enemy is getting weaker. Project AI Spirral is almost done."

"What can I do?" Andy asked.

Zoey, David, and Martha appeared next to him.

"You must break open that iron door. We will cover you with an invisible blanket for an hour so you can gain your strength back."

"Okay," Andy agreed.

Suddenly, he and his friends were covered by a blanket of invisibility. No one could see them, but they could see each other. The children felt the power around them.

"We have one hour to eat, rest, and get our strength back," Andy said.

"It's amazing," John added.

The time went very quickly, and Andy felt a burst of power fill his little body. He was almost glowing with a vibrant green light: the sages must have been beside them. With his knock spell, Andy opened the iron door. The heroes entered a huge room overflowing with computers that were giving off a deep blue light. The system looked alive.

"Who are you?" a harsh metallic voice called out.

"We came to claim the dark shield," Andy insisted.

Scary, deep laughter filled the room.

"Wimps like you? Do you really think you can get it?"

"We are no wimps." Andy raised his hand, ready to attack. John took out his two knives. Wendy also got her weapon ready and so did Zack. The rods sizzled in their hands.

"Then it will be a battle."

The moment the voice spoke, the floor started spinning counterclockwise. Then the room began to shift. Roller robots jumped at them quicker than expected. Yet, thanks to Wendy's foresight, she knew what was coming. The children stayed close together, striking each robot as it attacked. The room was raining with robot parts and burning sulfur that the children had to avoid.

Rods were sparking, rock balls were flying, and John's knives were slashing. Each strike took out a robot. The room filled up with screams of people who must have been lost in battles long ago. Several cries for help and strange noises filled the room. The party worked together to keep their balance and not fall into a huge hole that now surrounded them. They had nothing to grip on to; one false move, and it would be all over for any one of them. Teamwork was critical. The battle continued to rage on. Some robots had wheels and huge chains. Others carried rods, knives, and swords. The battle went on for several hours. The adrenaline kept the party strong. They realized they couldn't win without Andy's full support. When the deeper magic overtook Andy, everyone started floating above the room. It was as if a powerful twister had picked the children up.

Andy noticed a dark shape of a creature between two computers. Andy's gut feeling guided him. He knew that it was the target. He once again remembered the transportation spell. He closed his eyes in midair. It felt like something was keeping him from falling. He looked down at a woman's shape. In his head, he heard a voice: "I am sorry for all I did to you, Andy, back in Remake Academy. I will make things right again." Andy smiled for moment and remembered Miss Weed 2 torturing and humiliating him. Back then, she was not in control. She was on his side now. Without any further delay, Andy grabbed the mirror rod and wonder stone, focusing on the shield and his friends. The room got dark. The shield hit the rod head-on. It became part of the magical item instantly. The last thing he heard was Zoey screaming in his head.

He found himself and his friends just in front of the great structure again. The kids watched as the whole CORT Central factory collapsed into dust. Two people with sage symbols on their arms were standing in front of them.

"Thank you, Sage Andy and friends," the man greeted. He was wearing an orange robe.

"You did great, young man," the woman said. She was wearing a gray robe.

"Who are you guys?" Zack asked and fainted into Wendy's arms.

"We are the last two sages: Ellen and Kevin," they both said as one.

Just as the party was introduced, they felt exhaustion overtake them and everyone fainted to the ground. The heroes woke up in a large room. Martha was waiting for the party to wake up.

"Where are we?" Zack wondered.

"Great to see that you are finally well," Martha said with a smile. Next to her, Zack noticed two more people.

"What happened to us?" Wendy asked.

"We had to wake you using all of our powers," Martha explained.

"We thought we lost you," David added. "If it were not for Ellen, your quest would have ended."

"What do you mean?" Andy asked.

"You guys died," Martha said.

"How could that be? I did not feel a thing," John called out.

"Death has no pain: it is just the start of a new journey," David replied.

Andy could not believe that he died. Oh, how his friends would be jealous after he told them.

"Where are we?" Wendy asked.

"You are in a place called Field Temple," Martha stated.

"The home of the sages. I thought it only existed in fairy tales," John said.

"John, it was once a huge city before Icy City was built."

"It is where civilization began," David explained.

"How many years ago?" Andy asked.

"It was founded two million years ago," Martha said.

"Is this my home?" Andy looked at Zack.

"It could be if you wish."

"Are you crazy, Andy?" Zack responded.

"I will need to decide later, but first we have a mission to finish," Andy said.

"You have twenty-four hours before you must go to Iron Lady," Martha said.

"Where is Iron Lady?" Andy questioned.

"That is where you will destroy project Spirral."

"Is CORT Central gone?" Wendy interrupted.

"Yes, it is, thanks to you," Martha said.

"Are cities starting to wake up again?" Wendy asked.

"Yes, they are, Miss Wendy," Martha said happily.

"We have twenty-four hours to rest," Wendy told everyone.

"How about getting us some clothing?" Zack insisted. "Did you not notice we are all still naked?"

"Of course, Mister Zack," Martha said. She waved her hands and four one-piece white suits appeared on the kids. They fit perfectly. The children were escorted to their individual rooms for the night.

Chapter 20
Field Temple

It was hard for Andy to sleep because of all that had happened to him. He could not believe he died. It must have been some powerful magic. The room itself was simple with just one desk and a small lamp. The bathroom was at the end the hall and had to be shared with the floor.

He thought it must have been a dorm room, something that, one day, he hoped to be a part of. His whole life had changed that day he was swallowed by a portal. Andy felt like he had grown up a lot. Yet he still was just a boy with fantastic powers. Thinking about it made him feel so sad. What if his parents and friends forgot him? What if he would land in a different time? So much pressure on an eleven-year-old boy. With tears in his eyes, he fell asleep, and he knew his adventures were not over yet.

Two hours later, he woke up to a hard knock on his door.

"Who is it?" Andy asked.

"It is Wendy."

It didn't sound like Wendy. It must've been a trap, Andy thought. He pictured the pages of The Book of Know turning over. They stopped on a spell named "Reveal."

Perfect, he thought. He pronounced the spell aloud.

He saw an image of a very tall man behind the door.

"Are you okay, Andy?" the voice said. It still had that harsh tone to it.

"I will be right there, Wendy," Andy called out.

He quietly picked up the rod and pointed it toward the door. Suddenly, he heard a loud scream followed by a clattering sound. He opened the door. All he saw was a pile of ash.

Andy could not understand how a killer ended up here. Soon, his friends arrived.

"What happened here?" Wendy questioned.

John looked at the ash pile and understood what kind of creature had been destroyed. "It is a CORT shifter. It can transform into anything it wants to."

"How did it get here?" Wendy asked.

"They are very tricky," John said.

"They come in threes," Wendy added.

"Let's spread out," Zack said.

The children ran in different directions.

Will this ever end? Andy thought.

In total, the party took out six CORT shifters. They must have hidden in Field Temple when the place was empty. The party found several empty rooms here as they navigated the place. They sensed a lot of activity all around. The energy imprints were left behind.

Sometimes, intense heat overtook them. They smelled roses, daisies, and many other plants. Zack smelled death and fire in certain places.

After the hunt was over, they bumped right into Martha.

"What is going on?" Martha asked.

"Your old city was full of CORT shifters," Wendy explained.

"It is impossible: we have magic shields here."

"Your magic must have been destroyed," Andy said.

"We must all gather right away," Martha said.

"We will join you in fifteen minutes."

"You will find us in the main room."

"Where is it?"

"Second floor, fifth room on the right." Martha vanished.

"I sense the power is much greater than we know," Wendy told the boys.

"If we found six inside, how many of them are in the city?" John wondered.

"From what I understand, this place is huge," Wendy added.

"We must fight for our lives again. Nothing new for us," Andy said.

"You have to understand one thing: they can be anyone or anything," Wendy continued.

"So, we cannot trust anyone," John stated.

"We need to make a password," Wendy said.

"One moment, let me just use the Reveal spell one more time," Andy said. He took out his rod and scanned the room and his friends. The rod found three Shifters nearby.

At that moment, the three shifters transformed. One of them turned into a stone statue with four arms.

It moved fast toward Andy. When the shifter was five feet away, it swung one of its stone arms, just missing Andy by inches.

Andy raised his rod high. The wonder stone let out a dark purple light and instantly the stone sculpture shattered into a hundred pieces, covering the floor with gray rock dust.

The second shifter became a lion and jumped at Wendy, scratching her arm badly. Wendy moved fast, blood from her arm was pouring out on the floor. Just as the lion jumped for a final kill, she hit him right in the heart with a dagger. The lion screamed out in pain and collapsed in front of her.

The last shifter changed into a mechanical version of John. The battle took only five minutes since the creature lacked John's speed.

Zack had to work on Wendy right away or it would have been her end. He put his hands on her cut and thought back to the time he and his family were walking in Central Park. His emotions overwhelmed him. Zack's healing hands warmed up and healed Wendy quick.

"I have a feeling Wendy and Zack are in love," John whispered to Andy.

Zack and Wendy embraced each other and kissed.

"Oh, my goodness, it is true!" Andy called out.

"Yes, it is. Now you know our little secret," Zack explained.

The party stood in silence for the first time and looked at each other's faces. The moment of time was broken when Sage David emerged.

"This city is overflowing with evil. Guys, you must get out of here quickly," David insisted.

"Thanks, man. It is just a bit late," John said.

"Where are we off to now?" Zack asked, holding Wendy's hand, and looking at David.

"You must go to Iron Lady and save our world. We will clear things up here," David said.

"What is our mission again?" John asked.

"You all must seek and destroy Spirral. Do not forget that only with teamwork can it be done," David said and disappeared.

"More death traps most likely," Andy said.

"Nothing new for us, buddy," John said.

Andy still could not believe what he learned today. His geek brother had a girlfriend now. Andy hoped it would not ruin their plans to go home.

Chapter 21
Iron Lady

Martha and David helped the children to the north gate. As they navigated, they saw shifters everywhere. Andy hoped that one day soon he would be able to come back and see the beautiful city that now was in ruins.

"Goodbye, children," Martha said when they got to the gate.

"Will we see you again?" Andy questioned.

"I do hope so, my darling, but I never know." She gave kisses to each hero and vanished.

The party hoped they would see her again. They still did not know if Zoey survived back in CORT Headquarters. She never joined them here.

Andy was sick of all the death and suffering he had seen. He was happy his brother was with him, even though he fell in love with Wendy and talked less to him. John was a cool person. He was strange most of the time, but okay overall. He also was a little jealous of Zack, but happy that he got a girlfriend. As for himself, Andy had no time for one yet and it sounded a little icky to him to kiss a girl on the lips. One day, he would understand this boy-girl stuff, but not yet.

They were back in the wasteland for them and once again, the masks had to be put on.

According to what the sages told them; Iron Lady was about five miles away. Andy decided to hold back his magic because of the damage it might cause.

The winds had picked up and the feeling of a dark force approaching filled the air. Could they have gotten out too late? Was this the end of all they fought for?

Suddenly, they heard loud cries coming from nearby. Right in front of them was a small village. It was one street with a small square in the middle. A large robot with many iron arms was moving on the ground. Each arm had a weapon ready to be activated. As it moved, hissing and dark smoke came out of its mouth.

"Is it Spirral?" Andy questioned. "You think we can destroy it?"

"I think it is best if we hide," Wendy ordered.

"I agree. The only way to destroy a machine is to get rid of its source," John said.

The party slipped away and watched as this massive machine destroyed everything in its way. It seemed to get stronger as it moved. People were plowed down, structures fell like blocks, and plants evaporated. Luckily, it did not notice our heroes.

"What power does that machine have?" Zack said.

"We must do something!" Andy screamed out. He took off and pointed the rod toward the machine. It sparked and glowed but did not do any damage to the iron monster.

Andy was pulled back just in time because a missile started heading back toward him. It missed

Andy by three inches. Spirral's tail started swinging and its massive spikes hit the dirt Andy stood on just a minute ago.

"Look what you did," Wendy said.

"It has noticed us," John added.

Then two missiles exploded nearby. The party ran fast because at this point, they could not do one thing. They all felt hopeless.

"We should get back on the road. We can't do anything for this village," John said.

"We cannot let people die!" Andy screamed.

"You almost did, little brother," Zack reminded him.

"Martha told us we had to work as a team, and we must all remain alive to do that," Wendy interrupted.

It looked like there was no choice here. As John said, they had to find the source to destroy it.

"How much time do you think we have left before the big cities are hit?" Zack asked.

"The way that thing moves, we will be lucky if we have forty-eight hours left," Wendy said.

"Let's hurry to Iron Lady," Andy said.

"Do you think you can bring us there?" Zack suggested.

"I can try. Give me five minutes." Andy sat down on the floor and connected to his inner sage. Visions followed of a massive iron tower. It seemed to be floating above a lake. Andy mentally moved closer and saw the words "Iron Lady" above the tower. That had to be it. Using total inner peace and deep meditation, he imagined everybody in his party flying. Andy opened his eyes and placed the rod in front of him. His body started to feel light, and he was lifted into the air. Andy opened his eyes and discovered his friends were floating beside him. The landscape below moved fast. They flew over dirty roads, trees, and tropical plants. Everything below them glowed. They passed above small towns, huge fields, and tiny villages.

Andy could not believe they were flying. Was his magic that strong? All he learned seemed to fall into place like a puzzle that was finally finished. In three minutes, a large tower appeared in front of them. It did not seem to touch the ground at all. The sign, "Iron Lady," was in front of them. They landed right in front of the iron door, and it swung open for them as if the tower knew they were coming. Andy felt weak the minute they flowed in. The door slammed behind them and the party fell to the cold floor.

The huge hall was empty. The lights were turned on, and they noticed several massive hallways going in all directions. A strong wind slapped them. The Iron Lady was moving slowly in semicircles.

Andy felt so tired. All he wanted was to fall asleep peacefully.

"You must not sleep because you will never wake up," Wendy warned him.

"I must rest, or I am done."

"You must not." John slapped Andy on the face.

"Why did you do that?" Andy asked in a sleepy voice.

"I know what I am doing, and that is saving your life," John said.

"Nice one, little brother," Zack added.

"This will help you." Wendy handed Andy some fruit. The moment Andy took a bite, his body filled with energy once again. He felt wide awake.

"Thank you so much," he said.

"No problem." Wendy closed her eyes and scanned the tower. "It looks safe for us. The place had been emptied."

"It might have been but keep an eye out for traps and loose wires," John said.

"You mean it could be a trap?" Andy wondered.

"Yes, traps are common in places like this."

"Oh great," Zack said. "How does it move like that?"

"I think the whole place is a machine," Wendy said.

"Machines will do anything to protect themselves, always remember that" John said.

"You are saying Iron Lady is alive?" Zack said.

"It is kind of like that."

"How can a tower be living?"

"It should not be a surprise to you by now, big brother," Andy said.

"I guess you are right about that," Zack said.

Each step they took, the tower shifted more. John's foot hit a wire.

"Down, quick!" he yelled.

Arrows just missed everyone by inches, sticking to one of the upside-down walls.

"Watch out, man," Andy said.

"I did not see it," John said.

"One thing we all must do is look in front of us," Wendy said.

"Not only in front of us, but all around us," Andy corrected.

"Good point, since this place seems to be always moving," Wendy said.

The party continued moving through the tower, making sure nothing got in their way. Soon they found themselves in front of a massive iron door. The strange thing was that it was above them, and there was no ladder.

"Could that be it?" Zack asked as he took Wendy's hand and smiled.

"It probably is, darling," Wendy said as she kissed Zack on the lips.

"Please hold back the smooching. It is disgusting," Andy called out.

"Grow up, little bro, having a girlfriend is a part of life. I think you will learn that with time."

"Not in everyone's life, Zack," Andy said.

"He's got a good point. Many people never find anyone," John added.

"How about we find a way to get up there instead?" Wendy changed the topic.

Andy closed his eyes, and once again imagined the door opening and all of them floating inside. It was followed by a memory of his dog Buddy and parents back home. The long walks he took, the ball he played with him, and the many times he hugged him. Tears fell to the floor and the moment they hit, all four of them found themselves on the other side of the door. The Iron Lady stopped moving and the door banged closed behind them.

Chapter 22
<u>Spirral AI</u>

They found themselves in a massive room the size of ten football fields. They started to walk in the enormous space. Soon, the children realized that there were no walls and ceilings. They were moving through a forest polluted with used syringes, gloves, and white gowns. Scorched plants and rotten branches were everywhere.

"How could that be?" Wendy asked.

"I think we were deceived." Andy took out his rod and called out, "Show me your true shape, now!" Andy was correct: the forest vanished. They found themselves in a huge computer room. The moment it happened, flashing lights went off and heavy metal music started to play super loudly. The children's ears were about to burst.

Inside his head, Andy heard Zack's voice call out, "Stop this, bro!"

Andy raised the mirror rod high and faced it toward where the music was coming from. He watched as the music waves hit the dark shield and his rod, which reflected them back to the computer. This caused the wave to fly quickly and hit hard. The computers burst into flames and deactivated.

The room was thrown into complete silence. The lights continued to flash and, suddenly, the party heard a computer voice in their heads.

"Welcome to the war party." The children watched as all four sides of the room opened, and a flood of thirty robots started to roll out. They moved quickly into action.

"Leave it to us!" Wendy yelled out to Andy. "Your goal is to destroy the computer that is producing them." She raised her hands and our heroes jumped into action. They worked together perfectly, moving as one body and one mind. It was amazing to see how all his friends grew over the course of this adventure. Andy placed them in the back of his mind, closed his eyes, and pictured him walking his dog Buddy in the park. It was a beautiful spring day. The sun was shining, and the birds were singing. Serene feelings filled his body. He closed his eyes and went into a deep meditative state. "Show me the enemy!" A large computer with flashing rainbow colors appeared in the distance.

"Take me to it," Andy whispered. He felt his body levitate above the battlefield and float over. He woke up in front of a massive computer box.

"Andy!" the computer cried in his mom's voice, "you won't kill me, will you? Come, my son. How about a hug and kiss? I have not seen you in such a long time." The voices continued to change to different people's voices in Andy's life. Deep inside his heart, he knew everything was just an illusion.

"Connect to my inner spirit now," Andy said. At that moment, his brief life started flashing in front of him. All that was good and bad. All the suffering and sorrow. He was living it all once again.

Andy felt his body aching all over, and it happened as all his memories merged into one. The mirror rod slipped out of his hands and with all the force, crashed against the computer box. The whole room deactivated. Andy heard a door open somewhere. He fell to the ground and went into a deep sleep. He did not know how long he was out for. He woke up in the underground hospital. Joy was looking at him with her large smile and deep eyes.

"Welcome back, sleepy head," she said.

"How long have I been out?" Andy wondered.

He heard a familiar voice. "You have been out twenty-four hours." It was Wendy. Next to her were Zack and John.

"Did we do it?" Andy asked.

"Oh, we certainly did." John was wearing a large cast on his arm.

"You have brought peace back to our world," Wendy said.

"No, we all did," Andy corrected her.

"Soon, Icy City will be opening its gates for the people from all over this world," John explained.

Andy felt sad for some reason, as something was missing. He could not do magic anymore. "What happened to me?"

"Our powers have all vanished," Zack explained.

"Is it so?" Andy asked.

"They were just temporary," Wendy said.

Andy could not believe what he was hearing. He thought he would be powerful for the rest of his life. "How will we get home?"

"Do not worry about that, little bro," Zack said.

"Once the sages settle everything, they will bring you back home," John said.

"I have decided to come with you guys," Wendy added.

"Why?" Andy asked.

"She is interested in seeing our world," Zack said.

"We will tell you the details tomorrow. Now, sleep," Wendy insisted.

Andy did feel very tired and hungry. Before going back to his room from the hospital wing, he stopped in the kitchen and found a meal waiting for him. After eating his fair share, Andy went back to his room. He fell asleep thinking, *what will happen to us next?*

Chapter 23
Going Home

A ndy woke up early. He felt his strength had come back. He felt like a normal boy again. The amazing powers he once had were great, but now it was all over.

He wondered why this all happened. Were the brothers just pawns in a civil war? Why were they chosen for this job? On the one hand, Andy was happy it was all over, but on the other, it was sad. The time he spent on the quest was fantastic. He still did not understand why Wendy was coming with them. Did Zack want to introduce her to their parents? Was his brother going to get married so young? A million questions filled Andy's head. His thoughts were broken by a loud knock on his door.

"Hurry, David is here to give us a tour of the new world we have just saved!" Zack yelled behind the door.

Andy had never seen his brother so happy and excited at the same time. Soon the excitement charged Andy too. Zack did not say anything about Wendy.

Andy opened the door and there were Zack, Wendy, and David next to him.

"You guys did a great job," David praised them.

"Why were our powers taken away?" Andy questioned.

"You guys are going home soon, and those powers

will not be useful there. The mirror rod shattered and is gone."

"You are telling us that the mirror rod controlled our powers?"

"Just a part of them. The rest you did."

Things did make sense. Now what would they need such power in their world for? It was cool, but they were about to go back to a normal life anyway.

"You will see the transformed city from a plane, and your portal has been formed and activated. It will appear in about three hours," David said.

That was quick timing, Andy thought. *I guess it makes sense when four sages join forces.* The flight over the city was amazing. They looked out the window; a brand-new world was shown to them. Green foliage lined the streets, and glass skyscrapers kissed the sky. Green space and wildflowers were everywhere. It kind of reminded the brothers of a mini–New York City. It was awesome and alive again. A once empty city was beautiful again.

Wendy, Zack, and Andy looked at each other with huge smiles on their faces. What they did made them proud, and they knew that, because of them, a dying world was saved. Now they had amazing stories to tell their friends and family. They found the portal in Forest City; it was just starting to appear.

When the children landed, they were met by four sages. The first question Andy asked, where Zoey was.

"My darling boy, sadly, she was never found," Martha explained.

Sadness filled Andy's heart. He did not want to lose any of his friends, but he had. Hugs and thank you filled the field in front of the portal. The sages gave them a beautiful horn.

"This horn will connect us to you," Martha said.

"Please do not use unless an emergency happens," David added.

"Okay." Andy waved goodbye. Soon, a familiar buzzing noise appeared and once again, Zack, Wendy, and Andy entered the purple light.

Andy could not wait to see everyone. He had been gone for the longest time.

In a few minutes, the three children were spit out onto the street in front of the empty supermarket. Then the portal vanished once again.

Something did not look right. The supermarket was open, and downtown Trinity was full of potholes. "This is not our home," Andy said. The kids looked at the sky and saw four large lights fly by and disappear behind the clouds.

"This is not our home," Andy said.
The kids looked at the sky and saw four large lights
fly by and fade away into the clouds.

Acknowledgments

I would like to express my gratitude to the amazing team at Outskirts press for bringing my vision of "Spirral" to life. Thanks to my family for their full support but especially to my mom for doing an amazing job in editing this book. I also want to thank Mrs. Michele Sobel Spirn for her mentoring, guidance, and advice. I also want to thank all my local businesses both in White Plains and New York city for letting me write for many long days as I worked on this trilogy.

Illustrations

CPSIA information can be obtained
at www.ICGtesting.com
Printed in the USA
LVHW051501291021
701904LV00005B/108